EVANGELISTA'S FAN

Rose Tremain is a writer of novels, short stories and screenplays. She lives in Norfolk and London with the biographer Richard Holmes. Her books have been translated into numerous languages, and have won many prizes including the Orange Prize, the Whitbread Novel of the Year, the James Tait Black Memorial Prize, the *Prix Femina Etranger*, the Dylan Thomas Prize, the Angel Literary Award and the *Sunday Express* Book of the Year.

Restoration was shortlisted for the Booker Prize and made into a movie; *The Colour* was shortlisted for the Orange Prize and selected by the *Daily Mail* Reading Club. Rose Tremain's most recent collection, *The Darkness of Wallis Simpson*, was shortlisted for both the First National Short Story Award and the Frank O'Connor International Short Story Award. Three of her novels are currently in development as films.

ALSO BY ROSE TREMAIN

Novels
Sadler's Birthday
Letter to Sister Benedicta
The Cupboard
The Swimming Pool Season
Restoration
Sacred Country
The Way I Found Her
Music & Silence
The Colour
The Road Home

Short Story Collections
The Colonel's Daughter
The Garden of the Villa Mollini
The Darkness of Wallis Simpson

For Children
Journey to the Volcano

ROSE TREMAIN

Evangelista's Fan

& Other Stories

VINTAGE BOOKS
London

Published by Vintage 1999

4 6 8 10 9 7 5

Copyright © Rose Tremain 1994

Rose Tremain has asserted her right under the Copyright, Designs
and Patents Act 1988 to be identified as the author of this work

Some of the stories in this collection first appeared in the following
publications: 'Trade Wind Over Nashville' (*Pandora's Stories IV*,
Pandora, 1990); 'Over' (*Soho Square III*, Bloomsbury, 1990); 'Two
of Them' (*Marie Claire*, 1992); 'Ice Dancing' (*Telling Stories*, Sceptre,
1993); 'The Candle Maker' (*Trio*, Penguin, 1993); 'The Crossing of
Herald Mountjoy' (*Independent*, 1993); 'John-Jin' (Radio 4)

First published in Great Britain in 1994 by Sinclair-Stevenson

Vintage
Random House, 20 Vauxhall Bridge Road,
London SW1V 2SA

www.vintage-books.co.uk

Addresses for companies within The Random House Group Limited
can be found at: www.randomhouse.co.uk/offices.htm

The Random House Group Limited Reg. No. 954009

A CIP catalogue record for this book
is available from the British Library

ISBN 9780749396985

The Random House Group Limited supports The Forest Stewardship
Council® (FSC®), the leading international forest-certification organisation.
Our books carrying the FSC label are printed on FSC®-certified paper.
FSC is the only forest-certification scheme supported by the leading
environmental organisations, including Greenpeace. Our
paper procurement policy can be found at
www.randomhouse.co.uk/environment

Printed and bound in Great Britain by Clays Ltd, St Ives PLC

For the Romantic Biographer,
with love

Contents

Contents

Evangelista's
Fan

I

Salvatore Cavalli, the eldest son of a Piedmontese clock-maker, was celebrating his twenty-seventh birthday in the year 1815 when he learned that the King of Piedmont had decided to remove a large slice of time from the calendar.

This was disturbing news.

For several hours, Salvatore Cavalli's father, Roberto, had not been able to bring himself to pass it onto his son. He found the courage to do so only after he'd drunk several glasses of wine and eaten seventeen chestnuts soaked in brandy at the birthday dinner. Then, Roberto Cavalli wiped his mouth, put an eighteenth chestnut onto his plate, turned to his son, took a breath and said: 'Salvatore, I heard today that the King has ordered a number of years to be erased permanently from recorded time. What are we to make of that, do you think?'

Salvatore stared at his father. He wondered whether the clockmaker, a man of such precision in all his dealings, was beginning to show some inconsistency in his thinking. 'Papa,' said Salvatore, 'nobody can erase time. It's not possible. I think you must have misunderstood.'

But Roberto Cavalli had not misunderstood. With his mouth full with the eighteenth chestnut, he explained to Salvatore and to the assembled birthday guests that the King had been so horrified by the revolution in France and had suffered so miserably in his years of exile during the wars with Napoleon that he now preferred to pretend that none of these events had ever happened. His subjects were ordered to collude with this pretence and to purge their memories and their conversations of all reference to the years 1789 to 1815 inclusive. Punishments for disobeying the edict would be severe. Anyone heard uttering the word Bonaparte would be executed on the spot. The concept of *egalité* was decreed dead and had been officially interred in a dry well in the palace grounds. Worse and more difficult, nothing at all that had occurred during this time – *nothing at all* – was to be publicly recognised or discussed.

'So there it is,' said Roberto. 'The strangest decree ever to come forth, isn't it? And on this day of all days, my poor son. But there's nothing we can do about it. A decree is a decree and all we can hope is that we'll get used to it.'

That night, Salvatore refused to sleep. He stood at a window, counting stars. All twenty-six years of his life had been officially swept away. He existed only in the future – only from this moment of becoming twenty-seven – and all his past was consigned to a void, to a hole in time. He felt outraged. He came from a family whose profession it was to measure time, a family of rational, clever, mathematically-minded people. He found the King's decree absurd, adolescent, unhistorical, unscientific and untenable. He refuted it utterly. His father's cowardly acceptance of it infuriated him. He spoke to the stars, as they paled in the paling of the sky. 'I shall have to leave home,' he said, "leave home and leave Italy. Leaving is the only honourable solution left to me.'

Salvatore's proposed departure caused anguish in his family. He was already an accomplished assistant in the clockmaker's workshop. Roberto reminded him that their ancestors had started out as humble glass blowers but that for four generations they had been master craftsmen, rivalled only by the great watchmakers of France and Switzerland. 'You may *not* leave, Salvatore!' said Roberto. 'I forbid it. You are not free to abandon the family firm of Cavalli.'

'I have no other choice,' said Salvatore.

'Think of everything that has been done for you,' said Salvatore's mother, Magnifica, crying into a piece of Bavarian lace, 'the start you've had in life . . . '

Salvatore felt choked. He tried to stroke his mother's hair. 'There *was* no start, Mamma,' he said. 'I have no past. I am a day old.'

'Don't be stupid!' said Roberto, 'don't be pedantic.'

'I'm not being pedantic, I'm following orders. The years 1789 to 1815 have been cancelled.'

'In public, in public!' whispered Roberto, as if the King might be standing on the other side of the door, listening to the conversation, 'only in public! In private, they still exist. And this house is full of proof of their existence and yours, and these things can't be taken away: your baby curls in a box, your first prayer book, your tutor's reports, the engraving I gave you of the great Galileo Galilei, the first little clock you helped me make . . . '

'I can't live only in private, Papa,' said Salvatore, 'and anyway, I want to see something of the world.'

'Why?' asked Roberto. 'What's wrong with Piedmont?'

'Everything. A place in which time can be annulled and events denied and history rewritten is not a fit place to be and I pity you and Mamma if you're unable to see this.'

Salvatore felt pleased with this quick and pertinent response, but some days later, lying in the cabin of a ship that reeked of tar, hearing the sea boil all around him and knowing that Piedmont was lost to his sight, he heard the true harshness of his words and, for the first time, regretted them. He thought of Roberto and Magnifica alone with his absence, confused and afraid, and for a while he wished that the ship would turn round and take him back. But it sailed on.

His ultimate destination was England. Rumours had reached Piedmont during the wars that Napoleon had devised two alternative plans for the invasion of England: to fly horses and men and arms over in hot-air balloons; to dig a tunnel, like a mine, held up by wooden planks, under the

Channel, through which his army would pass. But his engineers had informed him that balloons were too fragile for the English wind and the earth beneath the Channel too crumbly for a mine, and so the schemes were abandoned and England had never become part of the Emperor's conquered lands.

It was because of this that Salvatore had decided to sail there. He didn't fear the windy climate. He thought that time, in an unconquered place, would be running normally. He had heard that the English were a finicky people, who did most things by the clock, and so he was confident that his skills would be in demand and that he could make his way in London.

He became quickly acclimatised to sea travel. He let Roberto and Magnifica go from his thoughts. The motion of the ships didn't make him sick; it filled him with a strange exaltation and sense of freedom.

At Lisbon, he fell into conversation with the ship's doctor, who spoke four languages and who began to teach him some words of English – earth, soul, city, morning, river, house, heart, bosom, Putney, ironmonger, fog – and proudly recited to him a poem in English about the beauty of London seen from Westminster Bridge which contained all but the last four of these:

> Earth has not anything to show more fair:
> Dull would he be of soul who could pass by
> A sight so touching in its majesty:
> This City now doth like a garment wear
> The beauty of the morning . . .

From this poem, once the Portuguese doctor had translated it for him, Salvatore formed an image of London as a place bathed in silvery light, a domed place, with silent ships at anchor and all its citizens at rest in the early dawn, watched over by well-oiled and perfectly adjusted clocks.

'I was right to leave Piedmont,' he said to the doctor. 'With the arrival of this new decree, my family skills will no longer be valued there. This follows logically.'

'Well,' said the doctor, 'I wish you success and I *expect* you to succeed. From my understanding of the English mind, I would say it has always been curious about contrivances and devices.'

Salvatore found premises in Percy Street. The previous occupant had been a bookbinder who had died quietly while resting from his labours in a leather hammock. Some of his books remained on a dusty shelf above Salvatore's workbench. He removed them to his bedroom (until such time as someone arrived to collect them) and forced himself to read a little from them every night, so that the language would enter him fast, like his mother's old cures for fever and melancholy, and make him strong.

He put up no sign. He had nothing, yet, to sell. And he needed, he believed, to understand the language and to know his way around London before he could start to trade there. He painted his premises green. He hung his precious engraving of Galileo Galilei over the mantel. This was to help him engage his future customers in conversation while they looked at his clocks and watches. He would remind them that it was an Italian, the great Galileo, who, observing very carefully the swinging of a lantern in Pisa Cathedral in the year 1582, had understood that the period of swing of a pendulum is independent of its arc of swing, and so adapted the pendulum to clockmaking via his simple idea of the wheel-cog escapement. He thought this story might be new to them and that it would intrigue and impress them.

Meanwhile, he began on the wheel-work of a range of 15-carat-gold keyless pocket watches, employing the Cavalli pump-winder patented by his grandfather, Domenico, in 1800. It was March and cold in his rooms. The kind of ferocious winds considered too fierce for Napoleon's hot-air balloons screamed at his door. There was no sign of spring anywhere. The silvery light he'd imagined from the poem on the ship didn't seem to fall in London except, now and again, just before dusk, just before the lamps were lit, and then it gleamed wetly on the street for half an hour and was gone.

And nor was London a gently sleeping city. Its very air seemed to hold noise within it, so that even while you slept you breathed it in and woke startled and disturbed. More even than the fiery Piedmontese, the men here seemed enraptured by argument and brawl. In Salvatore's own street, in the grey light that passed for broad daylight, he saw a man pick up a cat from the gutter and hurl this living weapon at the head of another man. The cat's body struck a railing and fell into a basement. The second man pulled out a pistol and shot the first man in the thigh. All down the street, windows opened and people stood staring. The wounded man lay pale and shrieking on the stones, but nobody went to his aid. After a while, he was put onto a cart of potatoes by some ragged boys and taken away.

That night, Salvatore dreamed that he'd lost not only his home but one of his legs as well. He got up and dressed and touched the great Galileo's forehead for luck and walked to Westminster Bridge and stood in the middle of it and tried to see the things spoken of in the poem. And, as it happened, the morning was a fine one, the wind less rowdy than of late. Spread out under a clear sky like this, the city did indeed seem beautiful and serene and Salvatore felt tall, as if he were at the centre of a picture. Then, he realised that from this heart of London, if a person turned very slowly in a 360° circle, his eye could come to rest on no less than thirteen public clocks.

His work on the watches progressed very slowly. He had never been a fast worker. (Would his father remember this and start to find his absence satisfactory?) But now, Salvatore's hands and his ingenuity felt constrained, as if he were, in fact, afraid to complete the watches. Certainly, he preferred wheel-work to enamel face-work. His numerals never satisfied him, never had the perfection he recognised in the internal machinery or the face pointers. So this, in part, explained why the watches remained unfinished, but not entirely, because he knew that his future was in them: he was nothing and no one, in his empty green shop, until he had begun to trade with the world outside.

It took him two months to understand the cause of his fear. It grew out of his personal predicament after the King of Piedmont's decree. He'd become uneasy about the validity of his profession. What did all this mathematical monitoring of time signify and what did it *serve*, if time could be mangled by the edict of a frightened monarch? He was in a country, now, where people seemed to pay proper attention to time, yet nevertheless he felt that, even here, his profession had been dealt some kind of blow from which – in his imagination – it might never recover fully.

It was May. The daylight was brighter, kinder, and Salvatore had made a few acquaintances now and went with them to the taverns and the coffee houses and spoke English and was less alone.

He went to a signmaker and placed an order for an expensive painted sign. It was to show a clock face with its glass casing cracked and its hour hand detached from the centre pinion. Underneath the picture, in black lettering, were to be written the words:

CAVALLI, S.   REPAIRER OF TIME

II

The wording of the sign made people stop and think and look up.

In the window of the shop, Salvatore had placed his unfinished watches and a set of sandglasses made by his ancestor, Vincente Cavalli, mounted in a fine ebony casing. He turned them every so often. He watched passers-by pause and stare at the minuscule movement of the white sand.

He wrote to Roberto and Magnifica: 'I have decided to specialise in reparation, rather than fabrication. This, I believe, will be better suited to my temperament and I will no longer have to disguise my ineptitude with face-work. My first task was to mend a Viennese table clock showing solar and lunar time by means of an astrolabe and delicate moon pointers. The pointers were jammed at the first phase, yet the moon here is full and overflows into the night mists. I say prayers for your understanding and forgiveness to this big, spilling moon.'

He prayed also that his business would thrive – and it did. 'A stopped clock,' said one customer, 'is a thing no Englishman can endure,' and it soon became apparent to Salvatore that his sign put Londoners in mind of the unendurable and they hurried to him in considerable numbers with timepieces of extraordinary diversity and differing complexity. People were, on the whole, polite to him. They made emphatic reference to his countryman, Galileo, there on the green wall. They spoke slowly and corrected his faults of syntax with good-natured courtesy. They paid promptly and greeted their mended clocks with affection, as though these might have been convalescent pets. Very occasionally, they returned with gifts of appreciation: an ounce of tobacco, a box of raisins, a lump of quartz.

It began to be clear to Salvatore that his decisions had all been right. He wrote again to his parents, from whom he'd received no word at all: 'I have begun to prosper a little in my new life.' At the same time, he felt that the life he had and which he referred to as 'new' didn't yet quite belong to him. It was like a coat he wore, a borrowed garment with holes in it, which let in, not cold exactly, but something mournful, something which sighed and should not have been there.

And then, on a late summer afternoon, a young woman walked into his shop. She was dressed in pale grey and white. There were white roses in her hat. Her hair was black (like the black hair of Piedmontese women in their youth) and her eyes were brown and of startling beauty.

Salvatore got up from his work table and bowed. Since arriving in London, his mind had been on language and on commerce; he'd given women hardly any thought. But now, suddenly in the presence of this person, he remembered how the sight of a particular woman could move him and terrify him at the same time, so that he'd feel exactly as he'd felt as a boy and imagined his life as a grown-up – wanting it and not wanting it, touched by possibilities, excited yet afraid.

In his still-imperfect English, Salvatore asked the woman how he might serve her. He thought that he saw her smile, but it was difficult to be certain, because on this warm day she had brought with her a fan and she held this fan, barely moving it, very close to her mouth.

'Oh,' she said, 'well, I've come as ambassador – ambassadress would be the correct term, but I think there are no ambassadresses on earth, are there? – for my clock.'

'Ah,' said Salvatore.

'It's a Dutch bracket clock, made by Huygens. The background to the dial is red velvet, slightly faded. The dial is brass and supported by a winged and naked figure of a man I've always taken to be God, or at least a god. It stands above the fireplace in my bedroom and I'm very fond of it indeed. A velvet background is unusual, isn't it? I couldn't say why I like it so much, except that it has always been there, ever since I can remember, ever since I could *see*.'

'And your clock is broken, Signorina?' asked Salvatore. He said this with great tenderness. His fear of the young woman had left him and only his longing remained.

'Well,' she said, 'it says twenty-seven minutes past one. It's paused there. The god still holds up the dial proudly, so it's possible that either he's showing me the time of the end of the world or else he hasn't noticed that his world has stopped. What do you think?'

Salvatore found much of this difficult to understand. He recognised a way of talking somewhat different from that of many young women, a kind of self-mockery in the speech, which he found seductive and he knew that she had asked him a question, but he really hadn't the least idea how to answer it. She looked at him expectantly for a moment, then smiled and hurried on: 'Take no notice of me! My mind is like a cloud, my father says, always drifting. And I expect it's because of my drifting mind that I've done what I've done. But it has upset me so much.'

'What have you done?' asked Salvatore, moving a step nearer to the young woman and snatching at the air with his nostrils to inhale more deeply a sweet perfume, which was either the smell of her body or the smell of the roses in her hat or a mingling of the two. She lowered her eyes. 'I've lost the winder key,' she said. 'I've ransacked the house for it. I've looked inside the grand piano – everywhere . . .'

Salvatore's eyes now rested on her small gloved hand holding up the fan. He wanted to take the hand and hold it against his face.

'. . . in every one of my shoes . . . in my father's pockets . . . under my bed . . .'

'But it has departed?'

'I believe it must be there, in the house, but no one can *see* it. There are certain things, of course, that are there and cannot be seen, but a winder key isn't usually one of them, is it? You come from Italy, I suppose?'

'Yes.'

'Italy is one of countless places that I've never seen, despite the fact that they exist and are there. But I have no doubt that Italy is more beautiful than almost anywhere on earth. Is it?'

Salvatore thought: I would like to go up into the sky with her, in a hot-air balloon, and float down on Piedmont, onto my parents' roof . . .

'I don't know,' he said, 'because I do not know the earth.'

At this moment, a church clock struck the hour of four and the young woman hurried to the door, saying that because her 'dear Dutch clock' had stopped she'd lost the race with time and was late for all her social engagements. She said she would come back the following day, with her servant to carry the clock, and Salvatore would manufacture a new key, adding before she left: 'Then all will be well again.' And after this, she was gone, adjusting her hat as she moved away down the street.

Salvatore sat down. He wiped his face with a handkerchief. He knew beyond any possible doubt – and indeed this knowledge seemed to be the only thing that was truly his since his arrival in England – that the young woman with the fan was his future. 'I shall marry her or die,' he said aloud.

She didn't return the next day as promised.

Salvatore had risen early, dressed himself with care, polished the glass of the engraving of Galileo Galilei and waited, but there was no sign of her.

After six days of waiting – during which he went out several times a day and walked up and down the street, searching among the heads of the people for the white roses of her hat – Salvatore told himself that he had misunderstood her. His grasp of English was still shaky, after all. She had not said 'tomorrow', she had said 'this time next week'. And he felt relieved and calmed.

So certain was Salvatore that she would come on this new tomorrow, that again he took extra care with his appearance, dusted the sandglasses and bought lilies from a flower seller to scent the green world of his workshop.

That same morning, he received a letter from his father. 'My dear son,' wrote Roberto Cavalli, 'by leaving the family, you have yourself tampered with time and continuity. Now, your mother and I feel cheated of our rightful futures and to console herself my beloved Magnifica is eating without ceasing and could die of this terrible habit, while I have no appetite for anything at all ...'

Salvatore wanted to write back at once to say that, when his future arrived, when – through his new idea of a marriage – he was fully able to inhabit his new life, then he would return to Piedmont, defying the King's edict by becoming responsible for the repairing of time, a skill for which he had now discovered himself well suited. But he didn't write. He sat at his workbench, waiting.

'Today, she will come,' he told himself, as the hours succeeded one another faster and faster. 'Today, she will come.'

Night came, that was all. And then another tomorrow and another.

Salvatore told himself: 'You are so stupid! Why didn't you ask for her name? Then you could find her. You could pay a respectful call, informing her that you'd come to collect the Huygens clock, to save her and her servant the trouble of the expedition. It would be perfectly proper. And then the key that you would make for her! What a key! Just to put it into the heart of the mechanism would be to experience a deep frisson of pleasure. And then to turn it! To set the escapement in motion! To know that time was beginning again ...' Salvatore knew that his thoughts were carrying him away, but he also believed that if he could only have the clock in his possession he could win the heart of the woman he now thought of as his future beloved.

He began work on designs for keys. Their heads had different emblems: a lyre, a rose, a pair of folded wings. He neglected other work to perfect them. And then, in the middle of the rose design, a realisation arrived in his mind like a canker in the flower: *she has found the original key!*

It was so simple, so obvious. She had opened the mahogany drawer where she kept her fans and there it lay. And so she had rewound the clock, set the pointers at the right time and given the matter no further thought. She would never come into his shop again. She was lost.

Salvatore put away his designs. He felt sick and sweat began to creep over his head. He remembered his father's letter and its terrible last sentence: 'I have no appetite for anything at all ...'

III

A feebleness of spirit overtook Salvatore from this moment. It was as if the King's edict had reached out to him, far away as he was, and annihilated him.

On the shop door, he put up a sign: *Repair suspended owing to illness.* From his bedroom window he watched the London summer glare at him and depart. He heard men rioting in the street below. They were shouting about the price of bread. Salvatore felt indifferent towards the price of anything.

In his more optimistic moments, he decided his extreme weakness was due only to exhaustion, to the difficulties he had had to endure since his arrival in London and his struggles with language. On other days, he felt certain that this new disappointment had dealt him a fatal blow. He noticed that his hair was starting to fall out. At twenty-seven, he hadn't expected this, just as he hadn't predicted that time could be wiped from the calendar. The capriciousness of the world was too much for the individual. However hard he fought to order his life, the random and the unforeseen lay in wait for him always.

He remained in his bed and didn't move. He ate nothing. He began to be prey to visions. He saw his lost beloved come into his room, naked except for her fan, which she held in front of her private parts. Then he woke one morning to the sound of someone eating. He saw his mother, sitting at his night table, spooning veal stew into a mouth that was much more fleshy than it had been, and he saw that all her flesh had magnified itself so grossly that her body almost filled the small room. He wanted to ask her why she had let this happen to her, but before he could frame the question, she said with her mouth full: 'It's my name. Magnifica. Why aren't you quicker to understand things?'

Salvatore tried to get out of bed. He wanted to lay his head in her enormous lap and ask her to forgive him. As he struggled towards her, he fainted and woke up lying on his floor, quite alone.

After this, he tried to eat. He nibbled at biscuits, felt deafened by the sound of them being broken against his teeth.

He put some pomade on his thinning hair. His scalp felt frozen, but he found that, under this ice, new thoughts were beginning to surface in his exhausted mind. The successful man, he decided, the man capable of a happy life, defies the random by his ability to *foresee* what is going to happen. He doesn't – as I have tried to do – feebly repair the past; his mind is attuned to what will *become* necessary. He acts in advance to prevent (as far as is humanly possible) the random from occurring. Such a man would have foreseen the possibility of the rediscovery of his beloved's winder key and asked discreetly for her name and address long before that possibility became a fact. Such a man, aware of the vanity of princes, would have predicted that the King of Piedmont was likely to attempt some wanton comedy with time and schooled himself as to how best to come to terms with it, so that he didn't have to feel as if his life had been cancelled. The random will still, of course, occur, but the damage caused to a life by the unforeseen will be less severe.

If only, if only, thought Salvatore, I were descended from a line of such men – men who possessed some cunning, not merely with the moment-by-moment measurement of the present, but also with the computation of the future – then I wouldn't be lying in this room in mourning for my lost love; I would be holding in my hands a Dutch clock. I would be working every hour of the day and night to make myself worthy of the woman I've chosen as my bride and who would one day be a bridge to Piedmont and the past. I would be happy.

The clarity of these thoughts consoled Salvatore for a time and then began to torment him. For why hadn't he had them sooner? They were no use to him now. They could only tantalise him with what might have been and now never would be.

He moved his bed. He put it under the window, so that he had a view of the street. He thought it would cheer him to watch the people hurrying by, each to his or her personal labyrinth of the unforeseen. He stared at the faces, so intent upon some destination, so certain of arrival. But instead of being cheered, Salvatore felt more and more sorrowful and ill. He experienced spasms of violent hiccups that hurt and exhausted him. After one of these, he had a vision of a fiery balloon floating down on London and so enthralled by this was he (was it there? was it not there except in his mind?) that he stopped looking at the street and began the habit of watching the sky.

The sky in England, he soon realised, was the most changeful and unpredictable thing of all. In Piedmont, a day that began fair stayed fair, or, if it didn't, the clouds gathered slowly in an orderly mass like an army and then marched in line towards the sun. Here, a morning could be fine for half an hour and then the sky could darken to night and a drenching rain start to fall and the temperature drop by several degrees. The poor English, thought Salvatore, they never know what's going to happen next in the sky. No wonder they're a brawling nation. They're venting a national rage against the utterly unfaithful seasons.

He became preoccupied with the weather. It was autumn now – two months since he had found and lost his beloved – and the sky was in a state of perpetual movement. He remembered sunny October evenings in Piedmont, sitting under a mulberry tree in Magnifica's garden when not a leaf moved and the day proceeded so calmly towards the night that it disturbed no one and no one noticed it go until it was gone. Here, the October dusk came flying in like a poltergeist, setting the shop signs swinging, rustling the leaves, sending smoke billowing back down the chimney in Salvatore's room, where he still lay in an enfeebled and pitiful state, his pillow darkened by his falling hair. With his mind swinging like a pendulum between the distant past in Piedmont (a past of long duration until it was obliterated by an external hand) and the recent past of his meeting with the only woman in his life who had ever truly moved him (a past of fleeting duration and obliterated by his own inadequacy), he felt himself begin to lose hold of earthly things. It was as if the air itself were snatching at him and wouldn't rest until it had whirled him up into the sky.

Some part of him, however, resisted. It refuted insanity, rebelled at the idea. It forced him to get out of bed, to shave his face, to comb his thinning hair. It dressed him in a black coat and sent him downstairs into the shop, where the dust was thick on every surface and now clogged the workings of the unfinished watches that still sat in the window.

Salvatore stared at all this. Pushed under his door were notes from customers demanding the return of their un-mended goods, the notes themselves curled and discoloured already by the passage of all the days since they'd been delivered.

Everything Salvatore could see appeared futile to him. He wanted nothing more to do with the reparation of time. His sign (he'd been so pleased with the wording on the sign, so proud of the little conceit!) now seemed to him a particularly stupid thing. He wished the wind had blown it down. Time could not be repaired. A sublime moment came and went and that was all. He was in a useless profession.

He ate a little food. He thought that to eat might help anchor him to the earth. All he had were some dried plums, but the taste of them was sweet and reviving.

To still his mind, he now fought to glimpse some small particle of his future. What in this world, he asked himself, can I do that will console me with its usefulness? What is there that is not futile?

He took his box of plums and went and sat by the mantel and looked up at Galileo. He tried to remember what the great man had done in *his* hours of adversity, in the last years of his life, when he was being overtaken by a terrible event beyond his control – his blindness. He had worked, with his son Vincenzo, on the pendulum-drive escapement. Salvatore imagined drawings discarded, half finished, covering his desk and Galileo's milky eyes so near the paper that he could use his long nose as a paperweight. He had fought his blindness to the last day and just three months before his death had been experimenting with mercury – a substance as volatile as time itself.

Salvatore ate another plum. He could feel his warm blood flowing in and out of his heart. Why mercury? What was Galileo doing – at terrible risk to himself because of his eyesight – with mercury?

The plums (a gift from a lawyer with a broken travelling clock) had some magical property. They seemed to revive in Salvatore a worm of optimism. They and Galileo's example. He sat there smiling, his mind tuned once more to answer its own questions.

He said out loud to the dusty shop: 'Galileo was working, in his mercury experiments, with Evangelista Torricelli. Three years later, Evangelista Torricelli designed the first barometer. The barometer remains one of the few scientific devices man has perfected that tell what is *going* to happen, not what is or what has been.'

At this point, Salvatore got up and took the engraving of Galileo from the wall and held it against his thin chest. 'This,' he said, 'is where a possible future might lie, then – with the barometer.'

IV

After his eating of the plums, Salvatore decided that, as soon as he was strong enough, he would go and talk to one of the numerous barometer-makers, whose premises he had often passed in his neighbourhood. Most of them had Italian names, but, afraid perhaps to discover that he had not been uniquely bold in coming to London, that London was in fact quite densely populated by refugees from Napoleon's wars, he had never visited any of them.

He eventually chose a shop in High Holborn. In the small window hung several wheel barometers. They were well-made pieces, but they were not the finest examples he'd seen. They demonstrated good craftsmanship rather than artistic delicacy and therefore mirrored Salvatore's assessment of his own skills. The name engraved on these instruments and over the door of the shop was FANTINO, E.

Salvatore entered the premises nervously. He hadn't worked out quite what he was going to say and he still looked pale and thin. He feared he would be mistaken for a student or a poet.

The interior of FANTINO, E. was dark. It smelled consolingly of resin and was warm. Salvatore felt as if he'd arrived in a place that he'd known long ago but had never had the words to describe.

A small, wiry man, wearing very thick spectacles, came out of an inner room. He stood at a tilted angle, peering at Salvatore. He said: 'I was about to say "good morning", sir, but I realise it may already be afternoon. When one is hard at work, one is apt to lose all sense of time.'

Salvatore nodded and gave the man an awkward smile. 'E vero, Signore,' he said. 'Si. E molto vero.'

'Ah!' said the tilted man, 'Italian! You are Italian!' And Salvatore noticed that a look of inexpressible joy passed over his small face.

'Si,' said Salvatore. 'And I have the honour, perhaps, to talk to Signor Fantino?'

'Oh no. No, I'm afraid not. I am Signor Fantino's partner in business, Mr Edwin Sydney. Signor Fantino is at present away, in Switzerland. But how may I be of assistance to you? We are always very glad to welcome your countrymen in our premises.'

The darkness and warmth of the shop, together with the friendly manner of Mr Sydney, gave Salvatore courage. He began at once to reconstruct, for the English partner of FANTINO, E., the tortuous excursions with time that had brought him to the barometer-maker's door. And the story, though long, seemed to enrapture the little Englishman. He stood with his eyes fixed on Salvatore's face, nodding, clasping his hands at intervals, as if filled with excitement. The tilt of his body became more and more profound and, at the point in Salvatore's narrative where he described the sudden entry into his memory of the name Evangelista Torricelli, Salvatore was afraid Mr Sydney was going to fall sideways onto the floor, just as the Tower of Pisa would one day.

When Salvatore reached the end of his story, with the words, 'and so, Mr Sydney, here I am,' Edwin Sydney said: 'If I were a religious man, Signor Cavalli, I would believe you had been sent to us by Divine Providence. Please step into our workroom and accept a glass of tea and I will call my cousin Mr Benedict Simpkins, who also works with me. We shall close the shop for the afternoon – it *is* afternoon, I now believe – and together we will discuss your apprenticeship to this firm.'

It was night when Salvatore returned to Percy Street. He made up a fire and sat in front of it, staring at the coals. The coals flared and burned and fell, burned and fell. And Salvatore's ability to reach a decision about his future followed a similar, repeating sequence. By morning, he was asleep in his chair, his mind still not made up.

Mr Sydney and Mr Simpkins had given him one month in which to accept or refuse their invitation. They told him that they would teach him everything they knew about the manufacture of barometers. ('Interest in weather forecasting began in prehistoric times, Signor Cavalli. Primitive man became aware of the concept of past and future and understood that his ability to ensure survival depended upon a sympathetic combination of sunshine, wind and rain.'). They would house him and feed him and nurture him back to his full strength. They would provide him with wine and tobacco and good paper for his letters to Piedmont. They would send out to a Piccadilly grocer for his favourite brand of dried plums. They would explain to him the ins and outs of bills of lading and all the paraphernalia of exportation. They would employ a teacher to improve his English. They would care for him, in short, like a son. But on one condition.

It was with his exhausted mind on this condition that Salvatore fell asleep in front of his fire. When he woke, cold and with an ache in his ear, he wondered whether he'd dreamed it up, so strange and unforeseen did it appear to him.

Sydney and Simpkins wanted him to disappear.

'Only for a short time, Signore,' they said, 'for as long as it takes you to become skilled with mercury, so that you can begin to follow in the footsteps of your countryman, Evangelista Torricelli. A year, say, or possibly nine months only. That will be up to you.'

The disappearance had to be absolute. No trace must remain of Salvatore, or of his watches, his repairs or his name at Percy Street. 'Your customers,' said Edwin Sydney, 'must be informed that you have returned to Piedmont. We will pay your landlord and close the lease. You must become absolutely invisible until you are forgotten.'

And then, when he had learned his new craft, when sufficient time had elapsed, he would be allowed back into the world. But not as Cavalli, S. As Cavalli, S. he would no longer exist. He was going to become Fantino, E.

'You mustn't think us mad,' said Benedict Simpkins, who was a larger man than Edwin Sydney, but with a slight facial resemblance to him. 'Necessity has made us act as we do. We've been looking for Fantino, E. ever since we began to trade in London.'

'But,' said Salvatore, 'where is he?'

'Ah,' said Simpkins, 'he is nowhere, Signor Cavalli. He has never existed. We invented him.'

Salvatore thought his comprehension of English must be failing him. He gaped at Simpkins.

'Yes, yes,' said Sydney, coming in quickly, 'we knew you would be surprised, but there you are. We made him up. We created him. And why? Because the Italians are the best barometer-makers in the world. They are *sans pareil.* That is an undisputed fact. Their reputation is paramount. So we invented the name Fantino. As you know, "fantino" is the Italian word for "jockey". And this was my first attempt at a livelihood, in the world of racing silks. You've· noted my stature, no doubt? But I was always a man fond of precision and the racecourse was, in the end, too uncertain a place for me. My cousin, Mr Simpkins, was at that time apprenticed to the firm of H. Hughes in Fenchurch Street and I joined him there. But we knew that when the time came to set up on our own, we would take an Italian name. We thought a mere name would suffice. But then we realised that we would feel more certain of our future if we had the man. And there you have it. Fantino, E. is trickery. It's a device. But why not? It's men's *devices* that shape the world. Don't you agree?'

Salvatore was silent. The two cousins smiled at him, smiled and smiled. These could have been the smiles of time-tampering kings.

'If I were to accept your offer,' he said at last, 'what would be my first name? What does "E" stand for?'

'Ah,' said Mr Simpkins, 'there our imaginations faltered and so we went straight to the originator of the Torricellian Experiment of 1643. It is, of course, Evangelista.'

After his sleep in the chair, Salvatore's mind felt a little more clear. I must lay out all the arguments in plain words, he thought. I must look at everything in a logical way and then make my decision.

He made coffee. He rekindled his fire and knelt in front of it, warming his hands on his coffee bowl.

He talked to himself as if he were no longer Salvatore Cavalli, but some disinterested third party. 'First,' he said, 'if you agree to become Fantino, E., you will also have the right to Fantino, E.'s constructed past as a maker of barometers. Your name is engraved on every instrument. The name, therefore, carries with it some years of prior existence that could go some way to redressing the balance of years lost as Cavalli, S. This is perhaps the most important point in the argument and one that should incline you to accept the proposal.

'Secondly, there is the name itself: Evangelista. This takes you yet further back, to a time of Italian greatness, to a time which acknowledged the vast importance of *prediction* in human life and addressed it scientifically. There is no more perfect assumed name for you, therefore, than Evangelista. Already you can feel the attraction, like a magnet, of this name.

'But then there is this third question of the disappearance. This disappearance means relinquishing for ever and always the possibility of your beloved's reappearance in your life. And, despite all your despair and suffering, you *have*, in some corner of your being, kept this possibility alive. You have said to yourself: suppose the winder key has *not* reappeared in the fan drawer? Suppose, simply, the bewitching owner of the Huygens clock (and don't forget that it was this very Huygens who perfected Galileo's escapement!) has temporarily become reconciled to the pausing of time at twenty-seven minutes past one? And suppose the day should come when this starts to irritate her once more? What will she do then? She will put on a grey dress (a winter dress this time). She will sew some silk roses to a hat. She will set out with her servant for Percy Street. And you will no longer be there. Worse, there will be no trace of you and no means whatsoever of finding you. She will take the clock to another repairer and that will be the end – the indisputable end – of any version of your future in which she is included.'

Salvatore sighed deeply. He put down his coffee bowl. He lifted his head and saw pale sunlight coming into the room. He realised that he could remember with extraordinary clarity the face, voice and gestures of the young woman he so yearned to love. She was as visible to him now as she had ever been. Nothing about her had faded or become spoiled. Her perfection remained intact, had imprinted itself indelibly on his mind. All she lacked was a name.

Thinking only of her and no longer of Fantino, E.,

Salvatore went to bed and slept away the morning. He dreamed he was walking arm-in-arm with his love in a field of string beans. The low bean plants touched his legs seductively. He woke in a state of frustration and fury. Come on, Salvatore, he instructed himself, you must put an end to this! Mr Sydney and Mr Simpkins have made you the most remarkable offer of your life and you must find the means to accept it. You must become Evangelista. You must make yourself relinquish love.

But how can perfection, once seen, be relinquished? It can't, Salvatore decided, it can't, because the mind will always and always return to it and all that follows will be measured by it – to the end of life.

Unless . . .

And here, Salvatore tried to remember how Sydney and Simpkins had described their creation of Fantino, E. They had called it trickery. They had said: 'It's men's *devices* that shape the world.' And this, of course, was what he needed now – a device. He had to behave not only like Sydney and Simpkins but also like the King of Piedmont: he had to invent a contrivance which, from the perfect sum of his love's whole, would take away a crucial part.

Some days passed.

Salvatore got out pen and paper. He stared at the paper for long hours at a time, absent-mindedly drawing designs for winder keys. Nothing in the way of any device would come into his mind.

One early morning, waking restless and confused, he put on his coat and walked through two rain showers and one deluge of hail to High Holborn and stood at the window of Fantino, E. The shop was not yet open. Salvatore remained there for several minutes staring at the instruments inscribed with his future name. Though not, as he had remarked before, as fine as many Italian pieces, the beauty of the barometers struck him more forcefully than it had at first. The face-work, done by Benedict Simpkins, was elegant, rather plain but nevertheless perfectly balanced, the word 'Fair' being particularly finely wrought. And Salvatore imagined himself returning to Piedmont at some future time with the gift of a barometer for Roberto and Magnifica. He saw the scene: Roberto would put on his spectacles and Magnifica would get up from the dinner table and they would both gather round and stare at the instrument and touch it and caress it and one of them would say at last: 'Well, son, the weaknesses you had as a clockmaker you have eradicated in this new profession of yours.'

These tender imaginings about his parents calmed Salvatore a little. If love could not make the bridge back to Piedmont, then perhaps the barometers would, in time.

He was able to set out on his return journey to Percy Street with a relatively tranquil mind. And then, on the way, something happened to him.

He passed a fan shop. Without really knowing why, he stopped in front of it and let his eye wander over the variety of fans displayed in the window. He was searching for a fan of decorated black lacquer, similar to the one his beloved had carried. There was nothing quite like it in the shop and Salvatore, beginning to muse on its singularity, suddenly understood that he had stumbled upon the device that would destroy his beloved's perfection. The device was her fan.

He remembered the encounter with her in every detail. And one of these details now struck him as immensely significant. Although the day had been warm, very warm, in fact, and the air muggy in his repair shop, the young woman had held the fan strangely still. One would have expected her to be fanning herself vigorously, but she was not doing so. In other words, despite the heat and humidity, *she had not used her fan like a fan.*

'And so,' said Salvatore, standing absolutely still at the fan shop window, 'she was not *using* the fan as a fan; she was using the fan as a device. It was a device of concealment, no less significant than that of Sydney and Simpkins and the invented Fantino, E. And what the fan concealed was a hole. In an otherwise ravishingly perfect oval face, there was a missing part. It was where a dimple might have been. It was a hole so deep, it had sucked in part of the cheek and all the skin at its rim was brown and puckered. It was a hole like an anus.'

Salvatore covered his eyes with his hands. A shower had come on while he had been standing at the window and he was now shivering with cold.

It took Salvatore two years (a year longer than Mr Sydney had anticipated) to re-emerge into the world as Evangelista. Mr Simpkins and Mr Sydney put this down to the young man's obsession with perfection. At first, this had exasperated them, but then they began to pay more and more attention to the quality of their own work, and the barometers made by the firm of Fantino, E. dating from the year 1818 surpassed in beauty and accuracy anything previously manufactured by them.

Their enterprise blossomed. Money was made. It was decided, in order to bind Evangelista more closely to the family, that he would marry Benedict Simpkins' daughter, Jane. She and any children born to her would take the name Fantino.

In the summer of 1820, after a protracted and happy visit to Piedmont, Evangelista was walking with his wife Jane in St James's Park when he saw, coming towards him, wearing a coral-coloured gown and a matching hat, the owner of the Huygens clock. It was a very warm day, but she carried no fan. She held her head high, seeming to smile at the fresh green of the park and the soft blue of the sky.

Her face was as beautiful and as untroubled by any imperfection as it had once been in Evangelista's Percy Street shop, and in his mind.

Evangelista noted this fact; then he reached for his wife's hand and walked on. Under his breath, he said his old name: 'Salvatore'.

The Candle Maker

For twenty-seven years, Mercedes Dubois worked in a laundry.

The laundry stood on a west-facing precipice in the hilltop town of Leclos. It was one of the few laundries in Corsica with a view of the sea.

On fine evenings, ironing at sunset was a pleasant – almost marvellous – occupation and for twenty-seven years Mercedes Dubois considered herself fortunate in her work. To her sister, Honorine, who made paper flowers, she remarked many times over the years: 'In my work, at least, I'm a fortunate woman.' And Honorine, twisting wire, holding petals in her mouth, always muttered: 'I don't know why you have to put it like that.'

Then the laundry burned down.

The stone walls didn't burn, but everything inside them turned to black iron and black oil and ash. The cause was electrical, so the firemen said. Electricians in Leclos, they said, didn't know how to earth things properly.

The burning down of the laundry was the second tragedy in the life of Mercedes Dubois. She didn't know how to cope with it. She sat in her basement apartment and stared at her furniture. It was a cold December and Mercedes was wearing her old red anorak. She sat with her hands in her anorak pockets, wondering what she could do. She knew that in

31

Leclos, once a thing was lost, it never returned. There had been a bicycle shop once, and a library and a lacemaker's. There had been fifty children and three teachers at the school; now, there were twenty children and one teacher. Mercedes pitied the lonely teacher, just as she pitied the mothers and fathers of all the schoolchildren who had grown up and gone away. But there was nothing to be done about any of it. Certainly nothing one woman, single all her life, could do. Better not to remember the variety there had been. And better, now, not to remember the sunset ironing or the camaraderie of the mornings, making coffee, folding sheets. Mercedes Dubois knew that the laundry would never reopen because it had never been insured. Sitting with her hands in her anorak pockets, staring at her sideboard, was all there was to be done about it.

But after a while she stood up. She went over to the sideboard and poured herself a glass of anisette. She put it on the small table where she ate her meals and sat down again and looked at it. She thought: I can drink the damned anisette. I can do that at least.

She had always considered her surname right for her. She was as hard as wood. Wood, not stone. She could be pliant. And once, long ago, a set of initials had been carved on her heart of wood. It was after the carving of these initials that she understood how wrong for her her first name was. She had been christened after a Spanish saint, Maria de las Mercedes – Mary of the Mercies – but she had been unable to show mercy. On the contrary, what had consumed her was despair and malevolence. She had lain in her iron bed and consoled herself with thoughts of murder.

Mercedes Dubois: stoical but without forgiveness; a woman who once planned to drown her lover and his new bride and instead took a job in a laundry; what could she do, now that the laundry was gone?

Of her sister, Honorine, she asked the question: 'What can anyone do in so terrible a world?'

And Honorine replied: 'I've been wondering about that, because, look at my hands. I've got the beginnings of arthritis, see? I'm losing my touch with the paper flowers.'

'There you are,' said Mercedes. 'I don't know what anyone can do except drink.'

But Honorine, who was married to a sensible man, a plasterer, shook a swollen finger at her sister and warned: 'Don't go down that road. There's always something. That's what we've been taught to believe. Why don't you go and sit in the church and think about it?'

'Have *you* gone and sat in the church and thought about it?' asked Mercedes.

'Yes.'

'And?'

'I noticed all the flowers in there are plastic these days. It's more durable than paper. We're going to save up and buy the kind of machinery you need to make a plastic flower.'

Mercedes left Honorine and walked down the dark, steep street, going towards home and the anisette bottle. She was fifty-four years old. The arrival of this second catastrophe in her life had brought back her memories of the first one.

The following day, obedient to Honorine, she went into the Church of St Vida, patron saint of lemon growers, and walked all around it very slowly, wondering where best to sit and think about her life. Nowhere seemed best. To Mercedes the child, this church had smelled of satin; now it smelled of dry rot. Nobody cared for it. Like the laundry, it wasn't insured against calamity. And the stench of calamity was here. St Vida's chipped plaster nostrils could detect it. She stood in her niche, holding a lemon branch to her breast, staring pitifully down at her broken foot. Mercedes thought: poor Vida, what a wreck, and no lemon growers left in Leclos. What can either Vida or I do in so desolate a world?

She sat in a creaking pew. She shivered. She felt a simple longing, now, for something to warm her while she thought about her life. So she went to where the votive candles flickered on their iron sconces – fourteen of them on the little unsteady rack – and warmed her hands there.

There was only one space left for a new candle and Mercedes thought: this is what the people of Leclos do in answer to loss: they come to St Vida's and light a candle. When the children leave, when the bicycle shop folds, when the last lacemaker dies, they illuminate a little funnel of air. It costs a franc. Even Honorine, saving up for her plastics machine, can afford one franc. And the candle is so much more than itself. The candle is the voice of a lover, the candle is a catch of mackerel, the candle is a drench of rain, a garden of marrows, a neon sign, a year of breath . . .

So Mercedes paid a franc and took a new candle and lit it and put it in the last vacant space on the rack. She admired it possessively: its soft colour, its resemblance to something living. But what *is* it? she asked herself. What *is* my candle? If only it could be something as simple as rain!

At this moment, the door of St Vida's opened and Mercedes heard footsteps go along the nave. She turned and recognised Madame Picaud, proprietor of the lost laundry. This woman had once been a café singer in Montparnasse. She'd worn feathers in her hair. On the long laundry afternoons, she used to sing ballads about homesickness and the darkness of bars. Now, she'd lost her second livelihood and her head was draped in a shawl.

Madame Picaud stood by the alcove of St Vida, looking up at the lemon branch and the saint's broken foot. Mercedes was about to slip away and leave the silence of the church to her former employer, when she had a thought that caused her sudden and unexpected distress: suppose poor Madame Picaud came, after saying a prayer to Vida, to light a candle and found that there was no space for it in the rack? Suppose Madame Picaud's candle was a laundry rebuilt and re-equipped with new bright windows looking out at the sea? Suppose the future of Madame Picaud – with which her own future would undoubtedly be tied – rested upon the ability of this single tongue of yellow fire to burn unhindered in the calamitous air of the Church of St Vida? And then it could not burn. It could not burn because there were too many other futures already up there flickering away on the rack.

Mercedes looked at her own candle and then at all the others. Of the fifteen, she judged that five or six had been burning for some time. And so she arrived at a decision about these: they were past futures. They had had their turn. What counted was the moment of lighting, or, if not merely the moment of lighting, then the moment of lighting and the first moments of burning. When the candles got stubby and started to burn unevenly, dripping wax into the tray, they were no longer love letters or olive harvests or cures for baldness or machines that manufactured flowers; they were simply old candles. They had to make way. No one had understood this until now. *I* understand it, said Mercedes to herself, because I know what human longing there is in Leclos. I know it because I am part of it.

She walked round to the back of the rack. She removed the seven shortest candles and blew them out. She rearranged the longer candles, including her own, until the seven spaces were all at the front, inviting seven new futures, one of which would be Madame Picaud's.

Then Mercedes walked home with the candles stuffed into the pockets of her red anorak. She laid them out on her table and looked at them.

She had never been petty or underhand.

She went to see the Curé the following morning and told him straight out that she wanted to be allowed to keep the future burning in Leclos by recycling the votive candles. She said: 'With the money you save, you could restore St Vida's foot.'

The Curé offered Mercedes a glass of wine. He had a fretful smile. He said: 'I've heard it's done elsewhere, in the great cathedrals, where they get a lot of tourists, but it's never seemed necessary in Leclos.'

Mercedes sipped her wine. She said: 'It's *more* necessary

here than in Paris or Reims, because hope stays alive much longer in those places. In Leclos, everything vanishes. Everything.'

The Curé looked at her kindly. 'I was very sorry to hear about the laundry,' he said. 'What work will you do now?'

'I'm going to do this,' said Mercedes. 'I'm going to do the candles.'

He nodded. 'Fire, in Corsica, has always been an enemy. But I expect Madame Picaud had insurance against it?'

'No she didn't,' said Mercedes, 'only the free kind: faith and prayer.'

The Curé finished his glass of wine. He shook his head discreetly, as if he were a bidder at an auction who has decided to cease bidding.

'I expect you know,' he said after a moment, 'that the candles have to be of a uniform size and length?'

'Oh, yes.'

'And I should add that if there *are* savings of any import . . . then . . .'

'I don't want a few francs, Monsieur le Curé. I'm not interested in that. I just want to make more room for something to happen here, that's all.'

Collecting the candles and melting them down began to absorb her. She put away the anisette bottle. She went into the church at all hours. She was greedy for the candles. So she began removing even those that had burned for only a short time. She justified this to herself by deciding, once and forever, that what mattered in every individual wish or intention was the act of lighting the candle – the moment of illumination. This alone. Nothing else. And she watched what people did. They lit their candles and looked at them for no more than a minute. Then they left. They didn't keep on returning to make sure their candles were still alight. 'The point is,' Mercedes explained to Honorine, 'they continue to burn in the imagination and the value you could set on the imagination would be higher than one franc. So the actual life of the candle is of no importance.'

'How can you be sure?' asked Honorine.

'I am sure. You don't need to be a philosopher to see it.'

'And what if a person did come back to check her individual candle?'

'The candles are identical, Honorine. A field of basil is indistinguishable from an offer of marriage.'

She had ordered six moulds from the forge and sent off for a hundred metres of cotton wick from a maker of nightlights in Ajaccio. The smell of bubbling wax pervaded her apartment. It resembled the smell of new leather, pleasant yet suffocating.

She began to recover from her loss of the job at the laundry. Because, in a way, she thought, I've *become* a laundry; I remove the soiled hopes of the town and make them new and return them neatly to the wooden candle drawer.

The Social Security Office paid her a little sum of money each week. She wasn't really poor, not as poor as she'd feared, because her needs were few.

Sometimes, she walked out to the coast road and looked at the black remains of what had been spin-dryers and cauldrons of bleach, and then out beyond this pile of devastation to the sea, with its faithful mirroring of the sky and its indifference. She began to smell the spring on the salt winds.

News, in Leclos, travelled like fire. It leapt from threshold to balcony, from shutter to shutter.

One morning, it came down to Mercedes' door: 'Someone has returned, Mercedes. You can guess who.'

Mercedes stood in her doorway, blinking into the February sun. The bringer of the news was Honorine. Honorine turned and went away up the street leaving Mercedes standing there. The news burned in her throat. She said his name: Louis Cabrini.

She had believed he would never return to Leclos. He'd told her twenty-seven years ago that he'd grown to dislike the town, dislike the hill it sat on, dislike its name and its closed-in streets. He said: 'I've fallen in love, Mercedes – with a girl and with a place. I'm going to become a Parisian now.'

He had married his girl. She was a ballerina. Her name was Sylvie. It was by her supple, beautiful feet that the mind of Mercedes Dubois chained her to the ocean bed. For all that had been left her after Louis went away were her dreams of murder. Because she'd known, from the age of eighteen, that she, Mercedes, was going to be his wife. She had known and all of Leclos had known: Louis Cabrini and Mercedes Dubois were meant for each other. There would be a big wedding at the Church of St Vida and, after that, a future . . .

Then he went to Paris, to train as an engineer. He met a troupe of dancers in a bar. He came back to Leclos just the one time, to collect his belongings and say goodbye to Mercedes. He had stood with her in the square and it had been a sunny February day – a day just like this one, on which Honorine had brought news of his return – and after he'd finished speaking, Mercedes walked away without a word. She took twelve steps and then she turned round. Louis was standing quite still, watching her. He had taken her future away and this was all he could do – stand still and stare. She said: 'I'm going to kill you, Louis. You and your bride.'

Mercedes went down into her apartment. A neat stack of thirty candles was piled up on her table, ready to be returned to St Vida's. A mirror hung above the sideboard and Mercedes walked over to it and looked at herself. She had her father's square face, his deep-set brown eyes, his wiry hair. And his name. She would stand firm in the face of Honorine's news. She would go about her daily business in Leclos as if Louis were not there. If she chanced to meet him, she would pretend she hadn't recognised him. He was older than she was. He might by now, with his indulgent Parisian life, look like an old man. His walk would be slow.

But then a new thought came: suppose he hadn't returned to Leclos alone, as she'd assumed? Suppose when she went to buy her morning loaf, she had to meet the fading beauty of the ballerina? And hear her addressed as Madame Cabrini?

And see her slim feet in expensive shoes?

Mercedes put on her red anorak and walked up to Honorine's house. Honorine's husband, Jacques the plasterer, was there and the two of them were eating their midday soup in contented silence.

'You didn't tell me,' said Mercedes, 'has he come back alone?'

'Have some soup,' said Jacques, 'you look pale.'

'I'm not hungry,' said Mercedes. 'I need to know, Honorine.'

'All I've heard is rumour,' said Honorine.

'Well?'

'They say she left him. Some while back. They say he's been in poor health ever since.'

Mercedes nodded. Not really noticing what she did, she sat down at Honorine's kitchen table. Honorine and Jacques put down their spoons and looked at her. Her face was waxy.

Jacques said: 'Give her some soup, Honorine.' Then he said: 'There's too much history in Corsica. It's in the stone.'

When Mercedes left Honorine's she went straight to the church. On the way, she kept her head down and just watched her shadow moving along ahead of her as, behind her, the sun went down.

There was nobody in St Vida's. Mercedes went straight to the candle sconces. She snatched up two low-burning candles and blew them out. She stood still a moment, hesitating. Then she blew out all the remaining candles. It's wretched, wretched, she thought: all this interminable, flickering, optimistic light; wretched beyond comprehension.

After February, in Corsica, the spring comes fast. The *maquis* starts to bloom. The mimosas come into flower.

Mercedes was susceptible to the perfume of things. So much so that, this year, she didn't want even to *see* the mimosa blossom. She wanted everything to stay walled up in its own particular winter. She wanted clouds to gather and envelop the town in a dark mist.

She crept about the place like a thief. She had no conversations. She scuttled here and there, not looking, not noticing. In her apartment, she kept the shutters closed. She worked on the candles by the light of a single bulb.

Honorine came down to see her. 'You can't go on like this, Mercedes,' she said. 'You can't live this way.'

'Yes, I can,' said Mercedes.

'He looks old,' said Honorine, 'his skin's yellowy. He's not the handsome person he used to be.'

Mercedes said nothing. She thought, no one in this place, not even my sister, has ever understood what I feel.

'You ought to go and meet him,' said Honorine. 'Have a drink with him. It's time you forgave him.'

Mercedes busied herself with the wax she was melting in a saucepan. She turned her back towards Honorine.

'Did you hear what I said?' asked Honorine.

'Yes,' said Mercedes, 'I heard.'

After Honorine had left, Mercedes started to weep. Her tears fell into the wax and made it spit. Her cheeks were pricked with small burns. She picked up a kitchen cloth and buried her head in it. She thought, what no one understands is that this darkness isn't new. I've been in it in my mind for twenty-seven years, ever since that February morning in the square when the mimosas were coming into flower. There were moments when it lifted – when those big sunsets came in at the laundry window, for instance – but it always returned, as night follows day; always and always.

And then she thought, but Honorine is right, it is intolerable. I should have done what I dreamed of doing. I should have killed him. Why was I so cowardly? I should have cut off his future – all those days and months of his happy life in Paris that I kept seeing like a film in my head: the ballerina's hair falling on his body; her feet touching his feet under the dainty patisserie table; their two summer shadows moving over the water of the Seine. I should have ended it as I planned, and then I would have been free of him and out of the darkness and I could have had a proper life.

And now. She was in Leclos, in her own town that she'd never left, afraid to move from her flat, gliding to and from the church like a ghost, avoiding every face, sunk into a loneliness so deep and fast it resembled the grave. Was this how the remainder of her life was to be spent?

She prised the buttons of wax from her cheeks with her fingernails. She took the saucepan off the gas flame and laid it aside, without pouring its contents into the candle moulds. It was a round-bottomed pan and Mercedes could imagine the smooth, rounded shape into which the wax would set.

She ran cold water onto her face, drenching her hair, letting icy channels of water eddy down her neck and touch her breasts. Her mind had recovered from its futile weeping and had formulated a plan and she wanted to feel the chill of the plan somewhere near her heart.

She lay awake all night. She had decided at last to kill Louis Cabrini.

Not with her own hands, face to face. Not like that.

She would do it slowly. From a distance. With all the power of the misery she'd held inside her for twenty-seven years.

Morning came and she hadn't slept. She stared at the meagre strips of light coming through the shutters. In this basement apartment, it was impossible to gauge what kind of day waited above. But she knew that what waited above, today, was the plan. It was a Friday. In Mercedes' mind, the days of the week were different colours. Wednesday was red. Friday was a pallid kind of yellow.

She dressed and put on her apron. She sat at her kitchen table drinking coffee and eating bread. She heard two women go past her window, laughing. She thought: that was the other beautiful thing that happened in the laundry – laughter.

When the women had walked on by and all sound of them had drained away, Mercedes said aloud: 'Now.'

She cleared away the bread and coffee. She lit one ring of the stove and held above it the saucepan full of wax, turning it like a chef turns an omelette pan, so that the flames spread

41

an even heat round the body of the wax. She felt it come loose from the saucepan, a solid lump. 'Good,' she said.

She set out a pastry board on the table. She touched its smooth wooden surface with her hand. Louis Cabrini had been childishly fond of pastries and cakes. In her mother's kitchen, Mercedes used to make him *tarte tatin* and *apfelstrudel*.

She turned out the lump of wax onto the pastry board. It was yellowy in colour. The more she recycled the candles the yellower they became.

Now she had a round dome of wax on which to begin work.

She went to the bookcase, which was almost empty except for a green, chewed set of the collected works of Victor Hugo and an orange edition of *Lettres de mon moulin* by Alphonse Daudet. Next to Daudet was a book Mercedes had borrowed from the library twenty-seven years ago to teach herself about sex and had never returned, knowing perhaps that the library, never very efficient with its reminders, would close in due time. It was called *Simple Anatomy of the Human Body*. It contained drawings of all the major internal organs. On page fifty-nine was a picture of the male body unclothed, at which Mercedes used to stare.

Mercedes put the book next to the pastry board, under the single light. She turned the pages until she found the drawing of the heart. The accompanying text read: 'The human heart is small, relative to its importance. It is made up of four chambers, the right and left auricle and the right and left ventricle . . .'

'All right,' said Mercedes.

Using the drawing as a guide, she began to sculpt a heart out of the wax dome. She worked with a thin filleting knife and two knitting needles of different gauges.

Her first thought as she started the sculpture was: the thing it most resembles is a fennel root and the smell of fennel resembles in its turn the smell of anisette.

The work absorbed her. She didn't feel tired any more. She proceeded carefully and delicately, striving for verisimilitude.

She knew that this heart was larger than a heart is supposed to be and she thought, well, in Louis Cabrini's case, it swelled with pride – pride in his beautiful wife, pride in his successful career, pride in being a Parisian, at owning a second-floor apartment, at eating in good restaurants, at buying roses at dusk to take home to his woman. Pride in leaving Leclos behind. Pride in his ability to forget the past.

She imagined his rib-cage expanding to accommodate this swollen heart of his.

Now and again, she made errors. Then, she had to light a match and pass it over the wax to melt it – to fill too deep an abrasion or smooth too jagged an edge. And she noticed in time that this slight re-melting of the heart gave it a more liquid, living appearance. This was very satisfactory. She began to relish it. She would strike a match and watch an ooze begin, then blow it out and slowly repair the damage she'd caused.

It was becoming, just as she'd planned, her plaything. Except that she'd found more ways to wound it than she'd imagined. She had thought that, in the days to come, she would pierce it or cut it with something – scissors, knives, razor blades. But now she remembered that its very substance was unstable. She could make it bleed. She could make it disintegrate. It could empty itself out. And then, if she chose, she could rebuild it, make it whole again. She felt excited and hot. She thought: I have never had power over anything; this has been one of the uncontrovertible facts of my life.

As the day passed and darkness filled the cracks in the shutters, Mercedes began to feel tired. She moved the anatomy book aside and laid her head on the table beside the pastry board. She put her hand inside her grey shirt and squeezed and massaged her nipple, and her head filled with dreams of herself as a girl, standing in the square, smelling the sea and smelling the mimosa blossom, and she fell asleep.

She thought someone was playing a drum. She thought there was a march coming up the street.

43

But it was a knocking on her door.

She raised her head from the table. Her cheek was burning hot from lying directly under the light bulb. She had no idea whether it was night-time yet. She remembered the heart, almost finished, in front of her. She thought the knocking on her door could be Honorine coming to talk to her again and tell her she couldn't go on living the way she was.

She didn't want Honorine to see the heart. She got up and draped a clean tea towel over it, as though it were a newly baked cake. All around the pastry board were crumbs of wax and used matches. Mercedes tried to sweep them into her hand and throw them in the sink. She felt dizzy after her sleep on the table. She staggered about like a drunk. She knew she'd been having beautiful dreams.

When she opened her door, she saw a man standing there. He wore a beige mackintosh and a yellow scarf. Underneath the mackintosh, his body looked bulky. He wore round glasses. He said: 'Mercedes?'

She put a hand up to her red burning cheek. She blinked at him. She moved to close the door in his face, but he anticipated this and put out a hand, trying to keep the door open.

'Don't do that,' he said. 'That's the easy thing to do.'

'Go away,' said Mercedes.

'Yes. OK. I will, I promise. But first let me in. Please. Just for ten minutes.'

Mercedes thought: if I didn't feel so dizzy, I'd be stronger. I'd be able to push him out. But all she did was hold onto the door and stare at him. Louis Cabrini. Wearing glasses. His curly hair getting sparse. His belly fat.

He came into her kitchen. The book of human anatomy was still open on the table, next to the covered heart.

He looked all around the small, badly lit room. From his mackintosh pocket, he took out a bottle of red wine and held it out to her. 'I thought we could drink some of this.'

Mercedes didn't take the bottle. 'I don't want you here,' she said. 'Why did you come back to Leclos?'

44

'To die,' he said. 'Now, come on. Drink a glass of wine with me. One glass.'

She turned away from him. She fetched two glasses and put them on the table. She closed the anatomy book.

'Corkscrew?' he asked.

She went to her dresser drawer and took it out. It was an old-fashioned thing. She hardly ever drank wine any more, except at Honorine's. Louis put the wine on the table. 'May I take my coat off?' he said.

Under the smart mackintosh, he was wearing comfortable clothes, baggy brown trousers, a black sweater. Mercedes laid the mackintosh and the yellow scarf over the back of a chair. 'You don't look as if you're dying,' she said, 'you've got quite fat.'

He laughed. Mercedes remembered this laugh by her side in her father's little vegetable garden. She had been hoeing onions. Louis had laughed and laughed at something she'd said about the onions.

'I'm being melodramatic,' he said. 'I'm not going to die tomorrow. I mean that my life in Paris is over. I'm in Leclos now till I peg out! I mean that this is all I've got left to do. The rest is finished.'

'Everything finishes,' said Mercedes.

'Well,' said Louis, 'I wouldn't say that. Leclos is just the same, here on its hill. Still the same cobbles and smelly gutters. Still the same view of the sea.'

'You're wrong,' said Mercedes, 'nothing lasts here in Leclos. Everything folds or moves away.'

'But not the place itself. Or you. And here we both are. Still alive.'

'If you can call it living.'

'Yes, it's living. And you've baked a cake, I see. Baking is being alive. Now here. Have a sip of wine. Let me drink a toast to *you*.'

She needed the wine to calm her, to get her brain thinking properly again. So she drank. She recognised at once that Louis had brought her expensive wine. She offered him a chair and they both sat down at the table. Under the harsh

45

light, Mercedes could see that Louis' face looked creased and sallow.

'Honorine told me you'd been hiding from me.'

'I don't want you here in Leclos.'

'That saddens me. But perhaps you'll change your mind in time?'

'No. Why should I?'

'Because you'll get used to my being here. I'll become part of the place, like furniture, or like poor old Vida up at the church with her broken foot.'

'You've been in the church? I've never seen you in there.'

'Of course I've been in. It was partly the church that brought me back. I've been selfish with my money for most of my life, but I thought if I came back to Leclos I would start a fund to repair that poor old church.'

'The church doesn't need you.'

'Well, it needs someone. You can smell the damp in the stone...'

'It needs *me*! I'm the one who's instituted the idea of economy. No one thought of it before. They simply let everything go to waste. *I'm* the one who understood about the candles. It didn't take a philosopher. It's simple once you see it.'

'What's simple?'

'I can't go into it now. Not to you. It's simple and yet not. And with you I was never good at explaining things.'

'Try,' said Louis.

'No,' said Mercedes.

They were silent. Mercedes drank her wine. She thought, this is the most beautiful wine I've ever tasted. She wanted to pour herself another glass, but she resisted.

'I'd like you to leave now,' she said.

Louis smiled. Only in his smile and in his laughter did Mercedes recognise the young man whose wife she should have been. 'I've only just arrived, Mercedes, and there's so much we could talk about...'

'There's nothing to talk about.'

The smile vanished. 'Show me some kindness,' he said. 'I

haven't had the happy life you perhaps imagined. I made a little money, that's all. That's all I have to show. The only future I can contemplate is here, so I was hoping—'

'Don't stay in Leclos. Go somewhere else. Anywhere . . .'

'I heard about the fire.'

'What?'

'The fire at the laundry. But I think it's going to be all right.'

'Of course it's not going to be all right. You don't understand how life is in Leclos any more. You just walk back and walk in, when no one invited you . . .'

'The church "invited" me. But also Madame Picaud. She wrote and asked me what could be done when the laundry burned down. I told her I would try to help.'

'There's no insurance.'

'No.'

'How can you help, then?'

'I told you, all I have left is a little money. One of my investments will be a new laundry.'

Mercedes said nothing. After a while, Louis stood up. 'I'll go now,' he said, 'but three things brought me back, you know. St Vida, the laundry and you. I want your forgiveness. I would like us to be friends.'

'I can't forgive you,' said Mercedes. 'I never will.'

'You may. In time. You may surprise yourself. Remember your name, Mercedes: Mary of the Mercies.'

Mercedes drank the rest of the wine.

She sat very still at her table, raising the glass to her lips and sipping and sipping until it was all gone. She found herself admiring her old sticks of furniture and the shadows in the room that moved as if to music.

She got unsteadily to her feet. She had no idea what time it could be. She heard a dog bark.

She got out her candle moulds and set them in a line. She cut some lengths of wick. Then she put Louis Cabrini's waxen heart into the rounded saucepan and melted it down and turned it back into votive candles.

Two of Them

Two of Them

We used to be a family of three: my mother, Jane, my father, Hugh, and me, Lewis. We lived in a house in Wiltshire with a view of the downs. At the back of the house was an old grey orchard.

Then, we became a family of two-and-three-quarters. I was fourteen when this happened. The quarter we lost was my father's mind. He had been a divorce solicitor for twenty years. He said to me: 'Lewis, human life should be symmetrical, but it never is.' He said: 'The only hope for the whole bang thing lies in Space.' He said: 'I was informed definitively in a dream that on Mars there are no trinities.'

My mother searched for the missing bit of my father's mind in peculiar places. She looked for it in cereal packets, in the fridge, in the photographs of houses in *Country Life*. She became distracted with all this searching. One winter day, she cried into a bag of chestnuts. She said: 'Lewis, do you know what your father's doing now?'

She sent me out to find him. He was on our front lawn, measuring out two circles. When he saw me he said: 'Capital. You're good at geometry. Hold this tape.'

The circles were enormous – thirty feet in diameter. 'Luckily,' said my father, 'this is a damn large lawn.' He held a mallet. He marked out the circles by driving kindling sticks into the

51

grass. When he'd finished, he said: 'All right. That's it. That's a good start.'

I was a weekly boarder at school. In the weekdays, I didn't mention the fact that my father had gone crazy. I tried to keep my mind on mathematics. At night, in the dormitory, I lay very still, not talking. My bed was beside a window. I kept my glasses on in the darkness and looked at the moon.

My mother wrote to me once a week. Before we'd lost a quarter of one third of our family, she'd only written every second week because my father wrote in the week in between. Now, he refused to write any words anywhere on anything. He said: 'Words destroy. Enough is enough.'

My mother's letters were full of abbreviations and French phrases. I think this was how she'd been taught to express herself in the days when she'd been a debutante and had to write formal notes of acceptance or refusal or thanks. 'Darling Lewis,' she'd put, 'How goes yr maths and alg? Bien, j'espère. Drove yr F. into S'bury yest. Insisted buying tin of white gloss paint and paint gear, inc roller. Pourquoi? On vera bientôt, sans doute. What a b. mess it all is. You my only hope and consol. now.'

The year was 1955. I wished that everything would go back to how it had been.

In mathematics, there is nothing that cannot be returned to where it has been.

I started to have embarrassing dreams about being a baby again – a baby with flawless eyesight, lying in a pram and watching the sky. The bit of sky that I watched was composed of particles of wartime air.

I didn't want to be someone's only hope and consolation. I thought the burden of this would probably make me go blind and I wished I had a sister, someone who could dance for my parents and do mime to their favourite songs.

When I got home one weekend, there were two painted crosses inside the circles on the lawn. They were white.

My father had taken some of the pills that were meant to give him back the missing part of his mind and he was asleep in a chair, wearing his gardening hat.

'Look at him!' said my mother. 'I simply don't know what else is to be done.'

My mother and I went out and stood on the white crosses. I measured them with my feet. 'They're landing pads,' said my mother, 'for the supposed spaceship from Mars.'

I said: 'They're exactly sixteen by sixteen – half the diameter of the circles.'

We sat down on them. It was a spring afternoon and the air smelled of blossom and of rain. My mother was smoking a Senior Service. She said: 'The doctors tell me it might help if we went away.'

'Where to?' I asked.

'I don't know where to. I don't suppose that matters. Just away somewhere.'

I said: 'Do you mean France?'

'No,' she said. 'I think he might be worse abroad. Don't you? And the English are better about this kind of thing; they just look the other way.'

'Where, then?'

I was thinking of all the weekends I was going to have to spend alone in the empty school. Sometimes, boys were stuck there with nothing to do for two days. A friend of mine called Pevers once told me he'd spent a total of seventeen hours throwing a tennis ball against a wall and catching it.

'What about the sea?' said my mother. 'You'd like that, wouldn't you?'

'You mean, in the summer?'

'Yes, darling,' she said. 'I couldn't manage anything like that without you.'

What I thought next was that it might be better to throw a ball against a wall for seventeen hours than to be by the sea with my father watching the horizon for Martians and my mother reminding me that I was her only hope and consolation.

I got up and measured the crosses again. I said: 'They're absolutely symmetrical. That means he can still do simple calculations.'

'What about Devon or Cornwall?' said my mother. 'They get the Gulf Stream there. Something might blow in. One can never tell.'

My father woke up. The pills he was taking made his legs tremble, so he sat in his chair, calling my name: 'Lewis! Lewis! Boy!'

I went in and kissed his cheek, which was one quarter unshaved, as if the razor had a bit of itself missing. He said: 'Seen the landing sights, old chap?'

'Yes,' I said. 'They're brilliant.'

'*Two,*' he said triumphantly.

'How did you know how big to make them?'

'I didn't. I'm guessing. I think there'll be two craft with four fellas in each, making eight. So I doubled this and came up with sixteen. Seems about right. Everything with them is paired, perfectly weighted. No triangles. No discord. No argy-bargy.'

I waited. I thought my father was going to tell me how the Martians could set about saving the world after they'd landed on our front lawn, but he didn't.

'What do they eat?' I asked.

My father took off his gardening hat and stared at it. 'I don't know,' he said. 'I overlooked that.' And he began to cry.

'It won't matter,' I said. 'We can drive into Salisbury and buy masses of whatever it turns out to be. It's not as though we're poor, is it?'

'No,' he said. He put his hat back on and wiped his eyes with his shirt cuffs.

My mother found a summer holiday house for us in north Cornwall. It was out on a promontory on a wild hill of gorse. From the front of it, all you could see was the beach and the ocean and the sky, but from the back – the way my bedroom faced – you could see one other house, much larger than ours. It was made of stone, like a castle. It had seven chimneys.

On our first day, I found a narrow path that led up from our house directly to it. I climbed it. I could hear people laughing in the garden. I thought, if I were a Martian, I would land on this castle roof and not on our lawn in Wiltshire; I would go and join the laughing people; I would say, 'I see you have a badminton net suspended between two conveniently situated trees.'

My parents didn't seem to have noticed this other house. Wherever they were, they behaved as though that spot was the centre of the universe.

On our first evening, they stood at the French window, looking out at the sunset. I sat on a chair behind them, watching them and hearing the sea far below them. My mother said to my father: 'Do you like it here, Hugh?'

My father said: 'Beach is ideal. Just the place. Better than the bloody lawn.'

That night, when I was almost asleep, he came into my room and said: 'I'm counting on you, Lewis. There's work to be done in the morning.'

'What work?' I said.

'I'm counting on you,' he repeated. 'You're not going to let me down, are you?'

'No,' I said. 'I'm not going to let anybody down.'

But then I couldn't sleep. I tried throwing an imaginary tennis ball against an an imaginary wall until the morning came.

We made circles in the sand. I was supposed to calculate the exact spot where the sun would go down, as though we were building Stonehenge. My father wanted the sun to set between the two circles.

My mother sat in a deck chair, wearing a cotton dress and sunglasses with white frames. My father took some of his pills and went wandering back to the house. My mother went with him, carrying the deck chair, and I was left alone with the work of the circles. They had to have sculpted walls, exactly two feet high. All that I had to work with was a child's spade.

I went swimming and then I lay down in the first half-made circle and floated into one of my dreams of previous time. I was woken by a sound I recognised: it was the sound of the castle laughter.

I opened my eyes. Two girls were standing in my circle. They wore identical blue bathing costumes and identical smiles. They had the kind of hair my mother referred to as 'difficult' – wild and frizzy. I lay there, staring up at them. They were of identical height.

'Hello,' I said.

One of them said: 'You're exhausted. We were watching you. Shall we come and help you?'

I stood up. My back and arms were coated with sand. I said: 'That's very kind of you.' Neither of them had a spade.

'What's your name?' they said in unison.

I was about to say 'Lewis'. I took my glasses off and pretended to clean them on my bathing trunks while I thought of a more castle-sounding name. 'Sebastian,' I said.

'I'm Fran,' said one of them.

'I'm Isabel,' said the other.

'We're twins,' said Fran, 'as if you hadn't guessed.' And they laughed.

They were taller than me. Their legs were brown. I put my glasses back on, to see whether they had a bust. It was difficult to tell, because their swimming costumes were ruched and lumpy all over.

'We're fourteen,' said Fran. 'We're actresses and playwrights. What are you, Sebastian?'

'Oh,' I said, 'nothing yet. I might be a mathematician later on. What are your plays about?'

'You can be in one with us, if you like,' said Isabel. 'Do you want to be in one?'

'I don't know,' I said.

'We only do it for fun,' said Fran. 'We just do them and forget them.'

'I don't expect I've got time,' I said. 'I've got to get these circles finished.'

'Why?' said Isabel. 'What are they for?'

'Oh,' I said, 'for my father. He's doing a kind of scientific experiment.'

'We've never met any scientists,' said Isabel. 'Have we, Fran?'

'We know tons of sculptors, though,' said Fran. 'Do you like sculpture?'

'I don't know,' I said. 'I've never thought about it.'

'We'll go and get our spades,' said Isabel, 'shall we?'

'Thanks,' I said. 'That's jolly kind.'

They ran off. Their difficult hair blew crazily about in the breeze. I watched them till my eyesight let them vanish. I felt out of breath – almost faint – as though I'd run with them into the distance and disappeared.

That night, my mother got drunk on Gin and It. She had never explained to me what 'It' was. She expected me to know thousands of things without ever being told them. She said: 'Listen, Lewis, the tragedy of your father is a tragedy of *imagination*. N'est-ce pas? You see what I mean, darling? If he'd just concentrated on the Consent Orders and the Decrees and so on, this would never have happened. But he didn't. He started to imagine the *feelings*. You see?'

She was scratching her thigh through her cotton dress. Some of the Gin and It had spilled onto her knee. 'So, listen,' she said. 'In your coming life as a great mathematical person, just stick to your *numbers*. OK? Promise me? You're my only hope now, darling, my only one. I've told you that, haven't I? So don't *start*. Promise me?'

'Start what?'

'What I'm saying is, stick to your own life. *Yours*. Just stay inside that. All right? Your mathematical life. Promise?'

'Yes,' I said. 'What does "It" stand for, Mummy?'

'What does what?'

' "It". What does it stand for?'

' "It"? It's just a *name*, sweetheart. A name for a thing. And names can make Mummy so happy, or so, you know . . . the other thing. Like your father, Hugh. Darling Hughie. Mostly the other thing now. All the time. So promise and that's it. Understood?'

'I promise,' I said.

The next day my father came to inspect the circles. Only one was finished. Just beyond the finished one was a sand sculpture of a bird. Fran and Isabel and I had stayed on the beach for hours and hours, creating it. They had made its body and wings and I had made its feet.

The bird was huge. It had a stone for an eye. My father didn't notice it. He was admiring the circle. 'Good,' he said. 'Now the other one. I'll give you a hand. Because the time's coming. I can feel it. I've been watching the sky.'

I worked with the child's spade and my father worked with his hands. The sight of his red hands scooping and moulding the sand made me feel lonely.

I waited all day for Fran and Isabel to come. At tea-time, it began to rain and I knew they'd be up in the castle, doing a play to pass the time. The rain fell on the bird and speckled it.

It rained for two days. My parents tried to remember the rules of Ludo. I walked in the rain up the path as far as the castle shrubbery, where I sat and waited. I stared at the droopy badminton net. I counted its holes. And then I walked back down the path and went into the room where my mother and father sat, and closed the door. They'd abandoned the Ludo game. They were just sitting there, waiting for me to return.

That night, I wrote a note to Isabel and Fran:

> Dear Isabel and Fran,
>   When is your next play? I would like to be in it, if you still want me to be.
> Yours sincerely,
> Sebastian

I set my alarm for four o'clock and delivered the note as the sky got light and the larks in the gorse began singing.

When the good weather came back, my father and I mended the circle walls beaten down by the rain. My mother watched us from her deckchair, wearing shorts. Her legs looked very pale. Sometimes, she went to sleep behind her glasses.

My father seemed restless and excited. He said: 'It's going to be soon, Lewis. And at night. I'm going to peg down two sheets in each of the circles. I've checked the moon. Visibility should be fair.'

'Good,' I said.

'I'm as prepared as I can be, thanks to you. Bar the food question. But your mother will cope with that. And there's always fish. Fish is a universal; it must be. But there's one other important thing.'

'What?' I said.

'You've got to be there. Your mother thinks this is a lot of drivel, so she won't come. So I'm counting on you. They want to see two of us. I'm as certain of that as I can be of anything. If there's only me, they'll take off again and go back to Mars.'

'Right,' I said.

But I wasn't really listening to him. My mind was on Isabel and Fran, who had sent me an answer to my note:

> Dear Sebastian,
> The first rehearsal for our next play
> is going to be in a tent we've pitched
> between our house and yours. Friday evening.
> Ten o'clock. Bring a glass.
> Yours faithfully,
> Isabel and Fran

Ten o'clock was the bedtime of our family of two-and-three-quarters. When we'd been three, it had been later. Now, my parents preferred sleep to life. In a dream, you can be transported back to pre-war time and find yourself dancing at the Café Royal.

I tried to imagine saying: 'Good night, Mummy. Good night, Dad. I'm going to a play rehearsal now,' but I couldn't. If you are the hope and consolation of anyone alive, you can't go to play rehearsals without warning.

So, I knew what I would have to do. I would have to wait until the house was silent and then creep out of it without being heard and find my way to the tent in the moonlight, remembering first to go into the kitchen and steal a glass. The thought of this made me feel very hot and weak. I sat down on the sand, with my arms on my knees.

'What are you doing, boy?' said my father.

'Resting,' I said. 'Only for a moment.'

I stood at my bedroom window. There was a thin moon. Bright but thin.

It was ten-eighteen by my watch.

I could hear my mother coughing. She said the cough came from the sea air.

At ten-thirty exactly, I let myself out of my room and closed my door. I stood on the landing, listening. There was no coughing now, no sound of anything.

I went downstairs, holding my shoes. I tried to glide soundlessly, like film stars glide into rooms.

I got a glass from the kitchen and unlocked the back door and went out into the night. I was wearing a grey shirt and grey flannel trousers and the things I could imagine most easily were all my grey veins going into my heart.

I moved up the path. I couldn't see the tent, but I could hear laughing – castle laughter. My mind seemed to be in holes, like a badminton net.

The tent was small. I'd imagined a kind of marquee. This tent was low and tiny. It was pitched on a little clearing in the gorse.

I bent down and called softly: 'Isabel? Fran?'

The laughter stopped. I could hear them whispering. 'I've come for the rehearsal,' I said.

There was silence. Then they giggled. Then Fran stuck her frizzy head out. 'You're late,' she said.

I began to explain and apologise.

'Ssh,' said Fran, 'sound carries. Come inside.'

She opened the little flap of the tent and took hold of my hand and pulled me in.

It was pitch dark in the tent and very hot. I felt blind. Fran said: 'Did you bring a glass?' Isabel said: 'Can you see us, Sebastian?'

There was a familiar smell in the little bit of air left me to breathe in; it was the smell of gin.

'You like gin, don't you ?' said Isabel.

'I don't know,' I said. 'My mother drinks Gin and It.'

They began giggling again. Now, I could see two soft white shapes, one either side of me. One was Fran and one was Isabel. They were wearing identical white nightdresses. Isabel handed me a glass of gin. She said: 'It's quite comfortable, don't you think? We stole masses of cushions. Try the gin.'

'And lie down,' said Fran. 'Relax.'

I took a sip of the gin. I felt it go into my veins.

I lay down, holding my glass in the air. I felt a hand on my face. I didn't know whether it was Fran's or Isabel's. The hand removed my spectacles.

'Don't,' I said.

'We've got to,' said Isabel.

'Why?' I said.

'That's the rehearsal,' said Fran.

'What do you mean?'

'Well,' said Fran, 'don't you want to rehearse?'

'You mean the play?'

'Yes. It's a kind of play, isn't it, Isabel?'

'Yes,' said Isabel.

'Except that there are two of us and only one of you and in the real future, when it's no longer a play rehearsal, it won't be like that. But it's OK, because we're so alike that in the dark you won't be able to tell which of us is which.'

'What do you mean?' I said. I let my glass tilt deliberately, splashing gin onto my face. The taste of it was beautiful.

They giggled. I felt the skirts of their nightdresses cover my legs, like feathers. Then I saw both their faces above mine and their crazy hair touched my forehead and my cheek.

'Come on, Sebastian,' they whispered. 'There's nothing difficult about it.'

I walked back to our house just as it was getting light.

From high up, I could see my parents on the little front lawn, wearing their dressing gowns and clinging together.

When they saw me, they stared at me in horror. Then my father broke away from my mother and came roaring at me. My mother followed, trying to catch him and hold him back.

'Hughie!' she screamed. 'Don't! Don't!'

But she couldn't catch him. He hit me on the jaw and I fell to earth.

I woke up in hospital, with a wire like a dog's muzzle round my face. I couldn't utter a word.

My mother was sitting by me. She looked pale and tired.

Later, she said: 'It wasn't only that we were worried, Lewis. There was the Martian business. He told me he saw them land. He saw them from his window. And he went running to find you and you weren't there, and then, as soon as he arrived on the beach, they took off again. He thought it was because there was only one of him. And then he was in despair. He felt you'd let him down and let the world down.'

I went back to school. I could move my jaw enough to say small words like 'no'. Autumn came.

My head had emptied itself of equations and filled up with the faces and bodies of Isabel and Fran.

My father went away. My mother wrote: 'They say it's just for a while, until all's well. But I know that the only *all's well* is you.'

The night after I got this letter, I had a dream. I was at home in Wiltshire, standing in the old, grey orchard.

I saw something come out of the sky and land on the lawn. It was a shadowy thing, without shape or measurable angle, and I knew what it was: it was my life and it was a thing of no hope and no consolation. I wanted to send it back into the clouds, but it stayed there, just where it was, blotting out all the further hills.

The Crossing of
Herald Montjoy

A piece of ground near Agincourt.
October 1415.

He does not have far to ride.

The distance between the two encamped armies is little more than a mile. They are so close that at night-time, in the cold stillness, each can hear the laughter of the other, and the swearing and the cries. They're like neighbouring farmers, eavesdropping in the moonlight.

The French are noisier than the English. There are far more of them, they have more liquor and they seem to know more songs.

Herald Montjoy walks out from the French camp, through the wood on the right towards Maisoncelles, and stands among the trees and listens to the English. He can hear a lot of hammering. He thinks the exhausted soldiers may be trying to make cabins out of elm. He remembers his little nephew, Roland, who has made a tree-house. He loves Roland. Having no children of his own, he's tried to describe what he is to Roland. He has told him: 'A herald is a watcher. It's important to understand this. He oversees the conduct of armies, but doesn't really belong to them. He's not a man-at-arms, but a man apart.'

Then, a morning comes, salt-white with frost, when Herald

Montjoy is summoned to the Dauphin's tent. The Dauphin instructs him to ride out across the fields to the English camp and enquire whether the English King is ready to ransom himself, to save his ragged army from certain defeat. The Dauphin's tent is sumptuous with blue and gold hangings. The Dauphin is doing body-building exercises all the while he is talking. As Montjoy leaves the tent, he hears him say to the Duke of Alençon: 'God, I'm fit.'

Herald Montjoy gets on his horse. The land he must cross has been ploughed and he's worried that the horse is going to stumble on the icy ridges of earth. A mist hangs on the fields, milky and dense, and the herald wishes that this, too, wasn't there. This and the hard frost give the day such strange singularity.

A piece of ground near the Manor of La Vallée.
April 1412.

He did not have far to ride.

The distance between his parents' house and the manor where Cecile lived was little more than two miles. He and his horse knew every step by heart. It was mostly downhill. And he would see the house long before he reached it. And always his thoughts flew ahead of him and landed, gentle as birds, on Cecile's head and on her shoulders and on her feet in coloured shoes.

She was so . . . *exceptional.* He tried, on these journeys to and from her house, to decide what, if anything, she resembled – in nature, or in man's inventions. He wondered whether he could compare her to a lake of water lilies where silvery fish glimmered deep down. Or was she like a sundial, unerring, yet always speaking, in her adoration of ephemeral things, of time's passing?

He decided there was nothing and no one as strangely beautiful as her. Not even the landscape through which he and his horse had to pass, with its flowering meadows, its clear stream, its silent woods and its perfumed air. Not even his dreams, in which he sometimes gave himself wings and flew up into the sky and floated above France.

No. Cecile was more to him than any of these things. She kept honey bees in tall hives in her father's orchard. Her beekeeping hat had a gossamer veil that fell to earth all round her, and whenever Herald Montjoy dreamed of flying above France, there below him walked Cecile in her bee-veil with nothing on underneath.

He knew he had to marry Cecile. He had to possess her: her body, her soul, her petticoats, her bees, her shoe cupboard. He couldn't wait much longer.

He was a handsome man, with dark soft hair and a curling lip, and he had no doubt that when he proposed to Cecile he would be accepted. He would say to her father: 'Sir, in two or three years' time, I aim to become Chief Herald of France. I do not think that is an unrealistic boast.'

> *Agincourt.*
> *October 1415.*

His hat is a strange confection, indigo blue with loops of velvet that fall just above his left eye and bounce up and down as the horse canters.

This bouncing of his blue hat as he advances into the icy mist makes him fret. It's as if everything is conspiring to blind him on this frozen day. He finds himself wishing it were night, with a round moon to light the field and the songs and the hammering of the English to guide him on. He feels that, under these conditions, he would see and think much more clearly; whereas, in this fog, with the forest petrified and silent close by, he feels confused and half-afraid.

He reins in his horse and turns him into the wood and dismounts. He sets down the weighty standard by an oak tree.

He ties the horse to the tree. He takes off his hat, runs a hand through his curly hair. All around him is the tracery of the night's frost, fingering every spine. He asks himself: Why afraid, Montjoy?

He is thirty years old, three years older than Henry of England.

Is everyone on this piece of earth afraid of the battle that is there and not there in every mind? Of the future battle that is coming or may never happen – there and not there, departing like a lover, returning like a fever?

The Dauphin isn't afraid. 'Afraid? Bunk!' And then he admires his leg. 'The English won't last more than half an hour. If that.'

His instructions reveal his nonchalance: 'Just tell the King to give himself up for ransom, all right, Montjoy? Then that sack of bones he calls an army can go home and litter up Southampton.'

He's been told to ride fast, to return quickly. The Dauphin's getting impatient with all the waiting. Montjoy has never disobeyed an order in his life, yet now he's in the wood, scratching his head, standing still, staring at the trees. He feels as if he can't make this crossing, but he doesn't know why.

La Vallée.
April 1412.

He felt weightless on that April morning. He felt as if he could swing himself up off his horse and into the air. He was wearing a sky-blue tunic. The sun shone on those soft curls of his.

He was riding to La Vallée to ask for Cecile's hand. His mother and father had waved and grinned as he'd set off: 'Such a *beautiful* girl, son. So striking! We wish you joy and success.'

His thoughts, as always, had already landed on Cecile. They

caressed her shoulder. They lay trapped like butterflies under her lavender-coloured cloak as she put it on and walked out of the house carrying a basket.

What was she going to put in the basket? Branches of blossom?

A thought is seldom trapped for long. It can travel anywhere. It can make decisions.

Montjoy's thoughts escaped from under the cloak. They walked with Cecile through the damp grass. They hid in the shadow of her skirts, high up in the darkness between her legs. They were touched in a caressing way as she took each step.

So then he had to slow his horse, dismount, walk to a stream, try to clear his head. 'You're running too fast,' he told himself. 'You're not her bridegroom yet.'

He knelt over the stream and cupped icy spring water and splashed his face. He gasped. There were days in a life so momentous they seemed to alter the size of the world. His heart felt as colossal as a cuckoo bird. The sky above his kneeling figure expanded and expanded, wider, fatter, closer to heaven than it had ever been.

He sat down on the grass. His horse grazed and flicked his tail at the spring flies. There *are* splendid lives, he thought. There *is* bravery and there is luck. There is ingenuity. A woman's shoe can be yellow . . .

There were yellow flowers at the stream's edge. Montjoy wasn't good at the names of flowers, but he sat there for a long while, admiring these particular ones.

Agincourt.
October 1415.

In this desolate wood, Montjoy looks for something green, something that will be soft to the touch.

This fear that he can't name has seeped from his mind, down and down all through him and touched his heart like

71

a ghost and then his sphincter, and now he's crouching down and defecating onto the dry bracken.

He can see nothing green, nothing soft to the touch to wipe his arse with. He has to scrape up handfuls of harsh bracken and fallen leaves and clean himself with these. As he pulls up his stockings, he feels like weeping.

The wood oppresses him. He'd come into the wood to find a moment's peace before he has to complete his ride to the English camp. But the wood feels dead.

Leaving his horse tied up and the standard leaning against the tree, he makes his way back towards the ploughed field under its curtain of mist.

He walks forward, his feet unsteady on the frosted ridges. He can sense, now, that the mist is going to clear and that the day may after all be fine. Already, there's more light on the field.

He looks down at the earth. He wonders who works this land, what crop he has in mind for the year to come. The loops of Montjoy's indigo hat fall over his eyes. He is standing now on the place where the very centre of the battle will be. Here, where his feet are, an English soldier will fall, his lungs pierced with a lance, blood bursting from his throat. All around him will lie his doomed compatriots, souls vanished into the air. This is the crop to come: in an ecstasy of death, this land will be seeded with the English. And it will be his task to count them – his and the English heralds' – to make an orderly tally, even if limbs or heads are severed and fall some way from the torsos. All heralds must be precise. They mustn't look away. Afterwards, he will say to his nephew, Roland: 'I saw it. It took place near the castle of Agincourt. But you couldn't call it a great battle. It was too one-sided.'

He is aware, suddenly, that a lot of time has passed since he set out. Far ahead, he can hear the English resume their pathetic hammering. And this comforts him, somehow. His fear has lessened.

He strides back into the wood and unties his horse. The horse is trembling with cold. He slaps it gently to warm it.

He mounts and takes up his standard. He faces his horse towards the light soaking through the rising mist and rides on.

La Vallée.
April 1412.

Sitting by the stream with the sun warm on his nose, Montjoy rehearsed his declaration of love and his offer of marriage.

He imagined Cecile standing with her back towards him, looking out of a window. He went down on one knee, but she hadn't noticed this. Her shoulders were very still. He said: 'Cecile, I think it must have been apparent to you for some time that I consider you to be the centre of my universe . . .'

He imagined her smiling – *so now he's going to propose to me!* – but trying to conceal the smile.

He said: 'And really so it is. Or rather, it's more than this: you have actually altered the way I see the world. Before I met you, my life seemed so small, so circumscribed. But together, you and I could become masters – or rather, I mean, master and mistress – of a fine destiny!'

He decided it was wise, or at least diplomatic, to ask Cecile at this point whether she, too, felt the earth transformed by *his* presence at her side. And he imagined that she turned from the window and came running to him and pulled him to his feet and said: 'Yes, Montjoy! Yes. I feel the earth transformed!' And then he kissed her.

The kiss was so heavenly that Montjoy, alone by the stream, let it last for several minutes. His eyes were fixed on some vacant spot, unseeing. Above him flew thrushes and finches. Fleets of minnows sailed by him in the water.

When the kiss was over, Montjoy looked around him. At dusk, he would ride back this way with Cecile's promise to be his wife locked inside him like money locked in a box. And always, after today, when he rode this way, he would feel that this was hallowed ground – the spongy grass, the yellow flowers, the icy stream – because it was here that his future came to meet him.

A bee buzzed by him.

He got to his feet. He and the bee were moving to the same enchanted, perfumed destination.

Agincourt.
October 1415.

One of their scavenge-parties, sent out to gather nuts and berries and firewood, sees him coming with his flying banner from far off. Two of the party stand and gape at him; two others start running back to the English camp.

They make him feel smart, these bedraggled English, carrying bundles of sticks. His blue hat no longer feels ridiculous, but slightly stylish. He bounces high in the saddle.

He is memorising the Dauphin's instructions: 'Look, Montjoy, the thing is perfectly simple. The English can't possibly win. We outnumber them five to one. If they can't understand this simple arithmetic, do a demonstration with pebbles or coins or any damn thing that happens to be at hand. They are about to be overwhelmed. What a marvellous word! *Overwhelmed.* I love it. Right?'

And now, as the mist disperses, he can begin to see the English camp. It huddles in among some thin trees. Just as he'd envisaged, the men have made themselves hovels from sticks and bracken. There are a few threadbare tents. Smoke rises from a dozen small fires. He can see soldiers grouped around them, trying to warm themselves. They turn their white faces towards him.

Montjoy has never been to England. He has been told that one corner of it lies under water, but that elsewhere there are great forests, older than time. And these men that he sees look half drowned to him, or else, with this pallor they have, appear like people who live perpetually in a wooded darkness.

He slows his horse. Like grey ghosts, English soldiers have crept out of the trees and stand staring at him. What honour for France can there possibly be in slaughtering people already half dead? What honour for the heralds to oversee such a massacre? He thinks of Roland. In the tender privacy of the boy's tree-house, Montjoy had once said to him: 'Roland, there are two things that have counted with me in my life and one of them is honour . . .'

But his thoughts are interrupted, because now he realises that a group of men-at-arms is approaching him. They have formed themselves into a square. In the middle of the square, Montjoy can glimpse something bright. It is the crown on the King's head.

Montjoy takes off his hat. He dismounts. Carrying the standard and leading his horse, he moves forward on foot. And in this moment (he can't say why) a fragment of his earlier fear lodges in his heart and he sees coming towards him, as if in a dream or a vision, not Henry of England but his beloved Cecile, wearing a garland of yellow flowers round her hair.

He falters. Then he urges himself on. He is aware, now, that hundreds of the English ghosts have come out of the trees and are gazing at him.

He bows to the King. When he looks up, he sees a squarish, bony face and a complexion less pale than those around him. The regard is soft and the voice, when he hears it, is gentle.

'Well, herald?'

'Sir,' says Montjoy, 'I've come from the Dauphin. He and all the nobles with him urge you to consider your position. They estimate that your army is outnumbered by five to one and they feel that, to save your men from certain death, the best course you can follow is to give yourself up for ransom . . .'

Montjoy sees one of the men-at-arms belch silently. He decides that two things keep these people from fleeing back to Calais: drink and the presence of their King.

'What is your name, herald?' asks the King.

'Montjoy, sir.'

The King smiles. The men-at-arms appear to stare through Montjoy at the piece of ground over which he has just travelled.

Still smiling, the King says: 'Montjoy, say this to Prince Dauphin. We would like to remind him that there are very few certainties on earth. Extraordinarily few. When I was a boy, I kept a stag beetle in an ivory box. I used to speak to it. And one evening, it spoke back to me. Until that time, I'd been absolutely certain that a stag beetle was unable to talk.'

The King laughs. The men-at-arms turn their anxious eyes from the field and look at their monarch.

'So you see,' says the King, 'one never knows.'

'What did the beetle say, sir?' asks Montjoy.

'Oh, I don't remember. Just a word or two. It was the unexpectedness that struck me. So there you are, herald. Your Dauphin can believe in his certainty or not as he pleases. It makes no difference to us. We will not be ransomed.'

The ghostly faces have clustered near to the King and are trying to listen to what he's saying. They stare and blink in the sunlight so foreign to them. They scratch their bodies through their clothing.

'God go with you, Montjoy,' says the King.

Montjoy bows. The King and his men-at-arms turn round and walk away. Montjoy replaces his blue hat on his dark head.

La Vallée.
April 1412.

There was the house. There were the doves, like winged thoughts, on the roof. Smoke drifted up from one of the stone chimneys.

Montjoy was still rehearsing his proposal as he dismounted and handed the reins of his horse to a servant. Then the servant informed him that Mademoiselle Cecile and her parents had gone to visit a cousin struck down by a tumbling weathercock. They were not expected back until late afternoon.

In the tableau Montjoy had seen in his mind, there had been *morning* light at the window where Cecile stood while he told her about the alteration to his world. And he liked things to proceed as he'd imagined them. So now he hesitated: should he leave or should he wait?

He decided to wait. The servant led his horse away. He sat on a stone wall and stared up at the sky. Then, he walked to the orchard where the apple blossom was in flower and stood near to Cecile's beehives. The traffic of bees to and from them absorbed his attention for a long time. He kept picturing the honeyed world inside. He decided that the thing in nature Cecile most closely resembled was a cluster of bees. She moved in ways that he couldn't fully understand and yet all the while there was purpose in her.

Cecile discovered him in the orchard. He'd fallen asleep in the sun and was dreaming of the sea. When he woke and found Cecile standing above him, he believed, for a fragment of a second, that she was a ship in sail, moving past him and on.

She was laughing. Montjoy realised how ridiculous he must look, asleep in the grass like a peasant boy. He scrambled to his feet, straightening his tunic, running a hand through his hair. Desperately, he searched for words.

Before he found any, Cecile held out her hands for him to take. He noticed then that her face was very pink and her eyes wide. She was wearing a white dress.

'My friend!' she said, 'I'm so glad to find you here! So happy! That you should be here – and sleeping like a child – is somehow perfectly right. Because I'm in such a state! You can tell just by looking at me, can't you? I'm in such a state of pure joy!'

77

'Are you, Cecile?'

'Yes! And you are just the person I want to share it with. You've been such a sweet friend to me and now I can tell you my wonderful news! What day is it? I'll always remember this day. Always and always. Now ask me why!'

'Why, Cecile?'

'Because Monsieur de Granvilliers proposed to me this afternoon. I'm going to be married! I'm going to have a wonderful life!'

Cecile let go of Montjoy's hands and went dancing off round the orchard, twirling her arms above her head. Montjoy saw that the shoes she was wearing that day were also white and it occurred to him that the grass would soon stain them. The grass appeared dry, but it wasn't. He could feel its dampness on his buttocks and against his shoulder blades and all down his spine.

Agincourt.
October 1415.

Returning at a canter, Montjoy soon leaves the smells and sounds of the English camp behind. He doesn't stop to look at the field or the wood. He isn't thinking about the battle to come, but about the kind of voice a stag beetle might possess. Up in his tree-house, Roland makes up different voices for the wind and the stars. Some of the stars don't speak, only yawn.

The Dauphin is at lunch with his favourite counts and dukes. They're eating blackbirds.

'God, Montjoy,' says the Dauphin, 'you've been an age. What happened?'

Montjoy is very hot after his ride. He can feel sweat in his hair.

'I'm sorry, sir,' he says. 'I explained to the King how far he's outnumbered, but—'

'But what?'

'He refuses to be ransomed. He seems willing to fight.'

The Dauphin picks up a blackbird and bites it in half, crunching the little bones. He speaks with his mouth full. 'Did you explain it properly? Five to *one*. Did you show him?'

'There wasn't an opportunity to show him, sir. His mind is made up.'

'Well then, he's a fool,' says the Dauphin. 'A bumptious fool. It means that he's now going to die. Simple as that. Every single one of them is going to die.'

The Dauphin eats the second half of his blackbird. He spits out a piece of bone and wipes his mouth. 'Get me the Constable of France, Montjoy,' he says. 'We'll get all this over with tomorrow. I'm tired of being here. And the food's ghastly. Off you go.'

Montjoy backs out of the Dauphin's tent. He feels tired. He feels he could lie down anywhere and sleep.

La Vallée.
April 1412.

Out of politeness, he had to pay his respects to Cecile's parents before he could leave. They told him that Monsieur de Granvilliers had hinted at his intention to marry Cecile back in January. Cecile's mother said: 'We're very flattered. This is a very good match.'

Montjoy wanted to say: I love her better than Granvilliers. She alters my earth. I'd sleep with her in my arms. I'd buy her any number of pairs of shoes.

But he kept silent and only nodded.

Then he rode back along the way he had come. The sun was going down and glinted red in the fast-running stream. He tried not to think of anything at all. When he got to the clump of yellow flowers, he looked the other way. His horse stumbled on a stone and he wished he could become that stone and feel nothing.

Montjoy's parents were eating dinner when he arrived back at the house. They looked up expectantly from their soup and put down their spoons.

Montjoy stood in the doorway and looked at them. For the first time in his life, he envied them with an aching, fathomless envy. They had lived side by side contentedly for thirty-one years. They still shared their bed.

He put a fist up to his mouth. Through the clenched fist, he said: 'Cecile's not in my life any more. So please don't mention her again. She's in the past and I don't want to speak about it. It or her. I don't want to talk about any of it. Ever.'

He turned and left the room before either his mother or his father could say a word.

Agincourt.
October 1415.

He has been summoned by the English King, three years his junior.

It's getting dark. The rain that came in the early morning has stopped and a white moon is rising. And under the white moon lie the French dead.

He and his horse have to pick their way among corpses. There's a shine on them and on the fouled earth where they lie.

For the second time in Montjoy's life, he asks himself, as he rides on into a gathering dusk: 'Why was something as terrible as this not foreseen by me?'

He remembers the Dauphin's mockery: 'They won't last half an hour!' He remembers his own imaginary words to Roland: 'You couldn't call it a great battle. It was too one-sided.'

He's a herald. Heralds ride in the vanguard of events. they announce. They watch and assess. They bring the expected after them. But not him. Despite his eminence, despite his optimistic name, the unimaginable follows him like a shadow.

He doesn't know precisely how this day was lost. He tried to follow what was occurring. He kept weaving in and out of the wood, trying to see, trying to get a picture. He heard the English arrows fly. He saw a cloud of arrows fall on the first line of cavalry, heard them clatter on helmets and backplates, like hailstones on an army kitchen. He saw some horses go down and their riders fall, helpless as saucepans in their armour, kicked or trampled by hooves.

Then he saw, as the first line rode on, the English men-at-arms fall back. They fell back in a ghostly way, just as, before, they emerged from the wood – one moment there and the next moment not there. And where they'd been standing, facing the French cavalry, on the very place where they'd been, now there was a line of stakes, newly sharpened, pointing out of the ground. There was a thick fence of them, a thousand or more, three or four deep with room in between them for only the most insubstantial men.

He knew the horses would rear, would try to turn, would do all that they could not to be thrown onto the stakes. But many of them couldn't turn because in their massed charge, flank to flank, they were coming on too fast and so they exploded onto the fence and their riders were pitched forward into the enemy's arms.

One of the other heralds had told him at dawn: 'The English are eating handfuls of earth. This means they accept their coming death and burial.' And he'd felt pity for them, as violent as love. Now, Montjoy's horse carries him awkwardly, slipping and staggering in the mud, through the field of the French dead. The dead appear fat with this white moon up, casting bulky shadows. Montjoy covers his mouth with his blue glove and tips his head back and looks for stars. There is one in the west, yawning, and he thinks again of Roland in his tree-house and then of all the souls of the French struggling to cross the chasm of the sky.

He won't give an account of the battle to Roland because

then he would have to answer too many unanswerable questions. Why did the first line of French cavalry turn round and collide with the men-at-arms coming forward? Does this mean that some of the French foot soldiers died before they even reached the English line? And then, when they reached the line, what happened that so many died so quickly? Were they packed together so tightly in a mass that they couldn't fight properly? Was the mass, shouting and pushing and afraid and confused, soon walled up behind its own dead?

It had rained so hard all through the battle, the heralds' task of seeing had been impeded.

All Montjoy can hope now, as he nears the English camp and hears voices singing, is thàt time will bring him understanding.

He rides on. He must make a formal acknowledgement of defeat to King Henry. He hopes that his voice is going to be strong, but fears that it may sound weak and small, like the voice of a stag beetle in an ivory box.

He feels exhausted. In his exhaustion, he aches to be no longer a man apart, but a man going home to his wife with a gift of crimson shoes.

The Unoccupied Room

Marianne is walking home through the wet dusk of the city. She wears an expensive grey mackintosh with the collar turned up, but she has no umbrella and her hair is cobwebbed with rain.

Marianne is forty-eight. She's an almost-beautiful woman who doesn't look her age. She has pale skin and a gentle laugh. She's a doctor specialising in geriatrics and her career is what matters to her now. She's divorced and unattached and certainly isn't looking for a new husband. Her only child, Nico, lives in another city. He's a radio DJ. Though affectionate to her always, she's heard him being condescending to phone-in listeners and she means to question him about this sometime: 'Why be cruel, Nico, when this isn't your nature?'

She carries a smart brown leather briefcase, inside which are her conference notes. This has been the final day of an international colloquium on geriatrics entitled 'Redefining the Seventh Age' and Marianne is aware, as the city traffic whispers by her on the damp cobbles, that she is, suddenly, exhausted. There's an ache in her thighs. Her eyes feel sore. She hasn't much further to go to her apartment, but she realises that she's been walking a long time and is surprised by the decision she must have made, but doesn't remember making, not to take a taxi home from the conference centre.

She could have afforded a taxi. Her ability to afford taxis now is one of the modest pleasures of her independent life. So why didn't she take one? She's walked at least a mile and her smart shoes are spoiled. Was it that she looked for a taxi and none came by? She doesn't remember looking for a taxi. All she remembers is that she was at the plenary session of the conference but said very little, or, perhaps, nothing, at it and that she is now here, three blocks or so away from her street. Her longing to be home, to make tea, to sit down, to warm her feet, has become overwhelming. She feels as though she could sleep for several days. She wants to lie down and not move and let nothing move within her sight or hearing, unless it might be a light autumn breeze at her window or the sound, far off, of the children's carousel in the park – familiar things that wouldn't disturb her peace. She sighs as she tries to hurry on. Her elderly patients have just such a longing for rest. 'I tell you, doctor,' says one old man, who sits at his window all day, counting aeroplanes, 'the best bit of the day is the night.'

She's at her street now. She turns off the well-lit boulevard and quite soon the traffic noise becomes faint and all she can hear are her own footsteps and all she can smell is the damp of the cherry trees that line the avenue. She likes this moment, this moving out of the light into the shadows of her street.

It's a street of nineteenth-century houses converted to apartments. Railings and hedges screen the ground-floor flats from the road. Only one house remains a house, containing thirteen rooms, but Marianne can't remember who lives in this grand building.

Her apartment is on the second floor. It has a large living room and three bedrooms, one of which is very small – the room Nico occupied as a child. The floors are polished wood, waxed often and scenting the whole place. It's the kind of apartment, unlike so many in the city, that you feel you can belong to.

Marianne searches in her mackintosh pocket for her keys.

She hopes they're in the pocket and not in her handbag, which has so many compartments in it that things lose themselves there. Her hands are soaking. In damp and cold, her nails, which she's bitten ever since she was nine, sometimes bleed. They feel as if they're bleeding now.

The keys aren't in Marianne's pocket, so she stops a little way from her front door, puts down her briefcase and places her handbag on someone's car roof, under a street lamp, to search for the keys.

At once, the contents of her handbag appear odd. She takes out something pale, slightly unpleasant to the touch. It's a pair of surgical gloves. In her day-to-day work, she wears gloves frequently (again and again she reminds the nurses: 'there must be a sterile barrier between your hands and all internal tissue of the patient's body'), but always disposes of them at the hospital or in the homes she visits. These gloves appear soiled and Marianne has never put a pair of soiled gloves in her handbag. Never.

She lays the gloves on the car roof. It's raining very hard now. She must find the keys, go in, make tea, sit down by the electric fire . . . Then, she will think about how the surgical gloves came to be in her bag.

The keys aren't where she expected them to be. They're at the very bottom of her bag. She has to take out her purse, her chequebook, her credit card wallet, her cigarettes, her tampon holder and her hairbrush before she's able to locate them. There's a label tied to them, on which is written *Keys No. 37*, but, just as Marianne has no recollection of putting the soiled gloves into her bag, so she has no memory of this label attached to her keys.

Her friend and colleague, Petra, reminded her some days ago: 'Conferences are strange things, Marianne. They're like stepping out of your life.' And now, as she returns her purse and the other items, including the gloves, to her bag, Marianne starts to wonder whether something has happened during the last three days, something she's momentarily forgotten because she feels so tired, that has damaged her.

She leans against the car, noticing that the car is dark red. A Volvo. It might belong to the family in the grand house, or it might belong to a woman on her own, gone shopping in the rain on the boulevard, a woman who found a lucky parking space here under the cherry trees. In one's own street, there are a thousand unknowable connections. Cities express the unknowable. Live your whole life in the same one and you will wind up a traveller in it, an ignoramus.

She's at the door of the building now. She pushes it and enters. The stairwell is massive, poorly lit, always cold. The stairs are stone, very wide, slightly grand. In the middle of this grandeur is an elevator no larger than a confessional, in which it has always been impossible not to feel foolish. Most often, Marianne ignores it and walks up the two flights of stone, but this evening she steps into it gratefully and lets it carry her towards her soft sofa, her fire, and the pot of China tea she's going to make.

It's dark in the apartment. Marianne switches on the overhead light and the hall seems brighter than normal. She rubs her eyes. She lets her bag and briefcase drop. She's aware, in the warmth of the apartment, that she's been enduring a headache for a long time without really noticing it.

Though she's been looking forward to the tea, she now feels too tired to make it. She goes straight to her bedroom. The bright light of the hall still feels uncomfortable, so she leaves her bedroom in darkness. She throws off her wet clothes and, wearing only a slip and a silk blouse, gets into the large bed she used to share with her husband, Paul. For fourteen years, they lay there together. On the living-room mantelpiece were stacked the invitations to conferences and poetry readings and private views and dinner parties: Paul and Marianne, Marianne and Paul.

Not that she regrets the passing of that bit of her life. Not at all. And now, as she feels a sweet sleep coming near, waiting, coming nearer, she thinks, not for the first time, I only endured it for so long for the sake of Nico.

* * * *

She knows she's slept for a few minutes but no more. She's warm. The pain in her head hasn't diminished. She lies very still.

She's been woken by something she can't identify. She raises her head, just an inch or two off the pillow, and listens. She can hear the rain on the window and the distant traffic of the boulevard. They're utterly familiar sounds and yet it seems to Marianne as if she hasn't heard them in conjunction with each other for a long, long time. It's as if there's been some vacant space between her and them. In a busy life, do you stop hearing the ordinary, the everyday? Or do you hear so much, so continuously, that half of it goes unregistered?

Marianne lowers her head onto the soft pillow. And she thinks, it was the past that woke me. I was dreaming about my parents, Otto and Lucie, dreaming myself back in our old apartment that smelled of pipe tobacco and cake baking. I was in my child's room and it was the sound I could hear from my child's bed that woke me up. It was one of those noises that used to come from the unoccupied room.

Marianne's room was at the end of the corridor. It had a small window that looked out over a courtyard, where a rusty fountain splashed during heatwaves and was silent the rest of the year. Hers was the 'last' room in the flat. The lives of their neighbours began on the other side of her wall. Their names were Joseph and Joanna Stephano. You could hear them from the bathroom, which was next to their kitchen. You could hear a kettle whistling and crockery smashing on the tiles and their voices shouting. (*'Why do they quarrel so?'* says Lucie. *'It's just their nature,'* says Otto.) But in her little bedroom, Marianne hardly ever heard them. So she'd worked out that the room next to hers was empty. It may have been a guest room where no guests ever came, or a fusty dining room that was never used, or even a box room kept closed and locked. And yet it had a function. Just one. It was where Joanna Stephano came to cry.

Marianne thinks, certain sounds from the past are never

forgotten. You come out of an important three-day conference and the crying of Joanna Stephano returns to you more clearly than the voices of the conference speakers. Once, it continued most of the night. You sat up and tapped on the wall, very lightly. You wished you'd learned Morse code so that you could send a message of consolation. At dawn, you heard Joseph Stephano start to call Joanna's name and, after that, you went to sleep.

But then. You heard something else. Later that same year or in the year that followed, when you would have been nine. Something that you never understood. Or did you? Was there an explanation which you once knew and have now forgotten?

It was a noise like a door creaking, a sound out of a Gothic tale. A creak, a squeak, wood against wood, wood against iron? Something opening, slowly, slowly. You heard it in the middle of the night. It woke you and you listened and you thought, what if the thing that's making this sound were to come through from the unoccupied room into my room?

Later – how much later? – Otto knelt down and held her and said: *'Try to forget it, Marianne.'* In fact, she remembers now, Otto and Lucie kept on saying this: *'Try to forget it, sweetheart. Put it out of your mind.'* But what were they talking about? Were they talking about the thing that caused the noise that night or about something else? What happened to Joseph and Joanna Stephano? Marianne is sure that in that building, somewhere in her childhood, there was another event. It took place on the stairs. Did it? On the dark stone stairs? If Otto and Lucie were alive, Marianne would call them up and they would remember, but Lucie has been dead for four years and Otto for two. Marianne is alone in her apartment. The time of families is gone.

Marianne is wide awake now. She decides she will go and make the tea, even eat something, perhaps, and then come back to bed, switch on the early evening news. She reaches out and puts on the bedside light. She sits up. The room is painted yellow. There are yellow and blue drapes at the window. On the opposite wall is an oil painting of a naked woman on a hard chair.

She looks at these things: the yellow walls, the curtains, the picture. She looks at the lamp she's just switched on. She looks at the book beside the lamp and the digital alarm clock on top of the book. She looks at the duvet, which is blue and white cotton.

This is not her room.

She remembers how her room looks. The walls are beige, the curtains white. By her bed is a photo of Nico.

This is not her apartment.

She is in bed in someone else's apartment. This is not even her city. It used to be her city, but it isn't any more.

Marianne fights her way out of the bed and snatches up her skirt. The digital clock on top of the book says 18.49. Along the boulevard, the traffic will be heavy now, bringing people home from their offices and one of these people will be the owner of this apartment. In moments, now, she will hear the elevator stop on the second floor and hear the rattle of the elevator grille.

The elevator . . .

Marianne pauses in her dressing. The elevator is hers. No. *Was once.* That feeling of foolishness. She knows the elevator like she knows her own car.

She's trying to straighten the bed. The bed is warm from her own body. Then she searches for her spoiled shoes. She's swearing under her breath to stop herself from crying. *Something has happened to send me mad. I'm as mad as a mad cow. I'm in someone else's apartment and at this very moment the owner of the apartment is parking her car under the cherry trees.*

Wait.

She knows the cherry trees. She knows the elevator. She had the keys to the apartment with a brown label attached to them.

Marianne wipes her face with her sleeve. She stares again at the room.

And then she sees it: hiding behind the yellow walls is the

ghost of her old room, the bedroom she shared with Paul for fourteen years. She had walked a mile through the rain, believing she was going home. She'd become, in a few hours, just like one of her patients who believe that a hospital ward is a university or a room in a sheltered house an Italian *pensione.* So she knows it now without any doubt: something has occurred in the last twenty-four hours to cause this damage. But she has no recollection of what it is. The one and only clue to it could be the surgical gloves.

She puts on her mac and grabs her briefcase. She goes out of the flat and slams the door behind her. As she tries to run down the stairs, she remembers how Nico used to race the elevator. But she hadn't really liked the game. She worried that he'd fall and gash his head on the stone.

She goes into the first café on the corner of the boulevard. She chooses a quiet table and orders coffee, not tea, and bread and soup and a glass of cognac. She asks the waiter to bring her four aspirin. The café is busy and she sits back on the banquette and closes her sore eyes and listens to the noise of conversation and laughter. She wishes her feet were dry and that the pain in her head would go. She remembers saying one day to Petra: 'I've always sympathised with the men and women in legends and fairy tales who sell their mules and their souls for trivial things.'

She could almost sleep, here in the warm café, lulled by arrivals and departures. But her food comes and wakes her. She takes the aspirin and begins on the soup, then the bread, then the coffee. She eats and drinks it all together – soup, bread, coffee, cognac. She can't remember when her last meal was or where.

When she's eaten and drunk everything, she leans back against the leather of the banquette and lights a cigarette. Out in the shadowy past, Otto, survivor of the death camps, says: *'People never think, when they're in a warm café, about the possibility of certain things. They don't consider that there could be bodies in the river, that bread could one day be scarce. To have these realisations, they have to go out into the street again.'*

Marianne will have to go out into the street again. She can't sleep on the café banquette, but by leaning against it she's located the source of her pain. There's a lump on the crown of her head and a scab of blood in her hair. At some time between the second day and the last day of the conference, she fell and hit her head or someone hit her. This, at least, it is now possible to assume. And there is also a second assumption. She no longer lives in this city and therefore must be staying at a hotel or with old friends. In her briefcase is her address book containing the names and addresses of all her friends in the world. Some are as far away as Japan and Australia, but most are still in Europe.

A man's voice, not Otto's, interrupts and says: *'I used to get off on Europe. You know?'*

An American voice?

And then?

A hand, broad, tanned, heavy. An expensive wristwatch with a platinum bracelet. She takes the hand in hers? The hand takes her hand?

The voice again: *'What are you doing, doctor? What the fuck are you doing?'*

Has she invented or dreamed the voice and dreamed the hand?

The food and drink and the aspirin and now the cigarette have soothed Marianne a little. It will be possible now – will it? – to search carefully through her bag and her briefcase, to find out where she's staying. Then she'll go there and sleep and hope to wake with her memory intact.

She calls out to the waiter. She's called so loudly, people in the café turn and stare at her. She has had to call above the angry American voice. *'Don't do this! Goddammit, don't do this to me!'* The waiter looks startled and comes to her at once. She orders more coffee and another cognac. She apologises for shouting. The waiter removes her soup plate. Marianne places her handbag on the café table.

There are eight small compartments in the bag. Marianne

searches them all. She finds three half-used books of matches, some Irish currency, a restaurant bill dated 19 April and a train ticket from Berlin to Brussels. There's no hotel key or key card. Her only discovery is that there is blood on the surgical gloves, more on the right-hand glove than on the left.

She drags her briefcase onto the seat beside her. She lights a second cigarette and snaps the case open. There is her conference file and on top of this a map of the city, un-opened. She used to live in this city and didn't believe she'd ever need a tourist's map. She used to park her car every night under the cherry trees.

Her coffee and cognac arrive. She opens the conference file and takes out her notepad. On the top sheet she's written, in a hand almost unrecognisable as hers: *In the US, an estimated four million people over 65 have diet-deficiency-induced abnormalities of bone matrix. Bones often fracture simply from body weight itself. People fall.* The rest of the page is blank except for some figure-of-eight doodles and two words: *cinema* and *Pieter.*

Marianne rubs her tired eyes. Pieter is one of her patients. Pieter sits on the balcony of the nursing home, painting watercolours of the sky, which he gives to her, one by one. About once a month, he begs her to sleep with him. He's ninety-one. Sometimes, he shows her his penis and tells her it is 'perfectly good'. She tells him gently that it's against the rules of the home for the doctors to sleep with the patients. She admires his sky pictures and brushes what's left of his hair.

He says: 'Being alone. You wait. You wait till you know what it is.'

'I *am* alone, Pieter,' she replies. 'It's my choice to be alone.'

'No,' he says, 'I mean really alone. You wait and see.'

Thinking about Pieter has frightened her. Not just the fact of Pieter and his life closing with these sad last requests, but something else. It has to do with the hand on hers, with the American voice. She has done something to Pieter. She's hurt or betrayed him in some way. Of this she is now certain.

She's still searching through the contents of her briefcase, but doing this absent-mindedly now. She wonders if she should call Petra. See whether Petra can explain to her what's happened, tell her what she's guilty of. *'Darling,'* says Petra softly, *'the past is always with us. At all times. It was you who taught me that.'*

Then, she finds it. A key to a hotel room. It has a number on it: 341. Marianne turns it in her hand. Modern hotel keys are plastic and operate a computerised lock. The name of the hotel is not on the key.

She struggles for an image of the hotel. A revolving door? A foyer with jewellery and scarves in a glass case? Staff in uniforms? But what comes to her is an amalgamation of all her journeys in Europe: a doorway in a Berlin street, a view onto a Paris courtyard, a Spanish room maid, the sound of a tram in Vienna. Petra seems to be with her in each of these places. *'Information,'* says Petra, *'is no longer a problem in the Western World. The sources of information are always somewhere to hand.'*

Marianne goes back to the conference file. Tucked into the conference notes is a letter of welcome from the organiser:

> Dear Conference Member,
>
> We are delighted to welcome you to our three-day colloquium, entitled 'Redefining the Seventh Age'. We hope that these three days will be rewarding and enlightening for all the participants.
>
> You will be accommodated for the duration of the conference at the Europa Hotel, which is situated two streets away from the Conference Centre (see map).

Marianne drinks her cognac. Why, she thinks, do certain drinks seem to warm your heart?

She finds a cab. Its interior is muddy, as if it were a water-taxi.

(Otto: *There is always, on a wet night in the city, some means of getting home, but every one of these nights, in our hearts, is a rehearsal for the night when there is no means and when there is no home to go to and we are the outcasts again.*)

The driver tells Marianne that he can't take a direct route to the Europa Hotel because one of the bridges is closed. A bomb has exploded at the central Post Office and the police have thrown a cordon round it. He will have to make a 'complicated' diversion.

'OK,' says Marianne.

He's a young man, quite eager to talk. He's worried about a letter he posted at five o'clock to his sister in Argentina. He says: 'It takes me all year to write to her. I don't know how to turn my life into words, that's my problem. And now my letter's gone up in smoke.'

On a different evening, in her own city, Marianne might have taken out a piece of paper from her briefcase and said to the driver: 'Let's write it again. You dictate and I'll put it down.' *Dear Maria, Don't faint. This is a letter from that marvellous correspondent, your brother. I am fine and hope you are and how are the Executive Boxing lessons going?* But tonight, she hasn't got the strength to be helpful in this way and decides, anyway, that the offer might be a patronising one.

They drive past the shuttered façade of a vast meat market, now closed while the city planners discuss new uses for it. 'I drove a film maker here,' says the driver. 'He was going to turn the meat market into an imaginary Finland. He told me he was famous, but if he was so famous why was he in my old cab?'

As they turn into a narrow, cobbled road in the oldest part of the city, the driver half turns to Marianne and smiles. 'I told you,' he says, 'a complicated route.' And Marianne sees that they're passing a row of shop fronts, lit and furnished like old-fashioned parlours and occupied by prostitutes who smile and pout and touch their breasts as the taxi goes slowly by. One of them, naked except for a red suspender belt and gold stockings, has fitted out her shop as an opulent bathroom and is sitting, legs apart, on a gold-plated lavatory. Marianne stares. The women in their little parlours amuse her, attract her, even. The girl on the throne shocks her. Yet she can't not look at her. She turns, cranes her neck, as the cab moves on.

'That one!' says the taxi driver. 'No shame, eh? They should make a law . . .'

'There's no law any more,' Marianne hears herself saying, and then, in the muddy dark of the cab, she sees, as if down a long tunnel, herself in a hotel bathroom. The suck of the extractor fan is hungry: *give me your foul air and I'll turn it into an icy breeze.* Marianne is taking off all her clothes and folding them into a neat pile. They're the clothes she's still wearing, the silk blouse, the skirt, the dark tights, the shoes now spoiled by the rain. And she's excited; sexually aroused and excited and nervous in her mind. She's going to sleep with a stranger. She, Marianne, who lives for her work with old people and for her son, Nico; she, who no longer dreams about past lovers or even about the touch of a man's hand on her hair, is going to go to bed with the tall American she met in the hotel bar. He has a large body. His hair is blond, but his pubic hair is dark. He works for a chemical company. She moves from the bathroom, holding her hands across her breasts, and sees him standing on the opposite side of the double bed. She wants him. She wants to lie down and be held close to his chest, to breath the half-forgotten smell of a man in her arms. She knows this is a moment of weakness, but she doesn't mind. But then. After he's undressed and she's undressed and they're standing face to face, she shivering a bit in the air-conditioned room, nothing proceeds as she wants it to proceed. The first terrible thing is the kiss . . .

'How are you going to pay?'

'What?' says Marianne.

'Is this a cash job?'

'What?'

'Cash or account, please? You got an account with the cab company?'

The taxi has stopped and the young driver is asking about the fare. They're at the Europa Hotel. Marianne recognises the entrance, but doesn't understand how they could have arrived here so quickly. Only seconds ago, they were passing by the prostitutes in their lighted windows.

'Cash,' says Marianne.

Then she pays the driver and gets out of the cab and is swept by the rain into the hotel foyer. She stands still in the bright circle of it. She can hear a pianist playing and realises that this is where it began, with the music in the bar, with some old sentimental tunes that reminded her of her life with Paul and even of her life with Otto and Lucie in that first apartment of all. It was the music that kept her there, ordering drinks, and which, after what seemed like a long time, made her angry to be so alone. And so she looked around and saw the yellow-haired American.

He'd been watching her. He told her that when they began to talk: 'I'd been watching you, but you're smart, you knew that, didn't you? I like mature women because you all know where it's at.' He had eyes that seemed gentle. 'What do you do?' he asked. 'I know you do something.'

'I'm a doctor,' she said. 'A geriatrician.'

He gave her this long, bleak look. 'My mother's old,' he said. 'Old is hell. Death is better. But I admire you. Let me raise a glass to all that you do.'

Marianne has no idea what time it is. It feels late. She finds her room key and walks to the elevator. She takes the elevator to the third floor and goes into Room 341. A switch near the door turns on an overhead light and a desk lamp. She puts down her briefcase on the desk. She looks around her. There's nothing of hers in the room: no suitcase, no books, no clock, no make-up bag, no perfume, no shoes or clothes, no photograph of Nico in its little perspex frame. The room appears unoccupied. It's the room of a guest who's already left.

Slowly, holding her arms round herself, Marianne moves towards the bathroom. She can remember now that when she got out of the bed, where she'd lain for so short a time, hurrying to her pile of clothes, the American followed her in there. *What are you doing, doctor? What the fuck are you doing?* She was trying to get dressed. The floor was slippery. He'd made her take a shower before he touched her. He'd showered, too. The marble floor of the bathroom was awash with water.

There are no possessions of hers in the bathroom. She knew there wouldn't be, yet she continues to search for them – behind the shower curtain, on the hook on the door, in the white pedal bin.

She was trying to get dressed and the American was yelling at her and then something happened.

In the pedal bin there is a piece of polythene packaging. Marianne looks at it. She takes it out and reads the label on it: *Yhoders Sterile Products Inc. N.Y. Gloves. One pair. Allsize.*

Marianne sits down on the cold floor of the bathroom. The fierce extractor fan seems to suck all the air upwards, out of reach of her breathing. She knows that she's probably, in the next quarter of an hour, going to be sick. She raises the lavatory lid. It feels suddenly dark in the bathroom. As in the taxi, Marianne sees herself small and far away, as though at the end of a tunnel.

It began with the kiss that was never a kiss. He said: 'In the old days, I would have kissed you, sure. But they're long gone. I don't employ my mouth any more. I'm sorry. No mouths. OK?'

He took her hands, as if to emphasise his apology for this, but then started to examine them and immediately noticed her bitten nails, one of which had bled recently. He left her standing there, cold, not kissed, not held. She crossed to the bed and tried to get in it, while he searched in his suitcase for something. He tore open the polythene package which contained the surgical gloves. He came to the bed and held them out to her and told her to put them on. 'Don't take offence,' he said. 'You could be Dr Death. How do I know?'

She should have left then. She didn't leave.

And there was a moment, she thinks, when he held her, when they held each other and she was warm and he stroked her thigh. But then he took one of her hands encased in its glove and guided it to his sex and said: 'OK. Make me want you.' He had no erection. 'Talk to me,' he said. 'Give me some cinema. I can't get it away in Europe any more. It's got dark here, or something. I keep trying, but no luck.'

He wanted her to talk about Pieter. She'd told him, down in the bar, drinking whisky, with the sweet music going on, that she had this old patient who kept offering himself to her and the American had laughed, had seemed to find it funny and tender and had let it go. But now he wanted her to arouse him with this, the story of Pieter: 'What does he do? Tell me what he does. God, even the dying have their brains in their pricks! Does he make you touch him? Does he masturbate in front of you?'

If she hadn't started to tell him, then there might have been something to save, despite his refusal to kiss her, despite the awful gloves, because she *wanted* it so badly after all her years alone. But, half drunk as she was, she did start to talk about Pieter and the American listened and became aroused in her hand and kept saying, 'OK, go on. OK, go on.' And then, suddenly ashamed – disgusted by her betrayal of Pieter, disgusted by her witless departure from a self she'd spent so long trying to become – she stopped talking and took her hand away. She picked up what she thought was her room key from the bedside table and got out of bed and went to the bathroom to put on her clothes and leave. She heard him start to yell at her. She was trying to take off the hateful gloves when he arrived in the bathroom. 'Hey! What are you doing, doctor? What the fuck are you doing? I was getting hard! Look! I've been in this stinking Europe for ten stinking days and this is the first time I feel like a man and not like a corpse and you're walking out on me!'

Marianne said nothing. She gave up on the gloves. All she wanted was to be far away from here. She knelt down by her pile of clothes and tried to put on her bra. He kept shouting. *'Words, of course,'* said Otto, *'can feel like stones, as if a building has begun to fall down all around you.'*

And then a sudden darkness came on.

* * * *

Marianne flushes the lavatory and closes the lid. She washes her face and hands and wipes them with a clean towel. As a child, she vomited often. Lucie was almost always with her, to comfort her, to hold her forehead and hold back her long hair.

She feels better. Almost weightless. Now she must go down to the desk and tell the receptionist she's mislaid her room key.

She returns the glove packaging to the bin and the soiled gloves with it. What else did he leave behind which the room maid saw and cleared away? Her own blood on the floor? What did her head strike when he kicked out at her? The rim of the bath or the underside of the washbasin? How long did she lie in his bathroom? She has no recollection of returning to her own room, but she knows it was there that she woke up, there that she got dressed, as if sleepwalking into her clothes, and set out for the final day of the conference. And all day she sat listening to the speakers but didn't hear them. She went to the platform to take part in the plenary session, but said nothing. All day, she'd been dreaming of going home to her beautiful apartment above the cherry trees.

She is given a key. Her room is two floors above his. The view of the city is grand and when Marianne looks down she can see the Post Office, still burning. All around it, blue lights flash.

She remembers there used to be fires in the city when she was a child. In those days, the fire engines rang bells. Lucie used to say: *'There's the fire bell, Otto,'* as the trucks passed.

There had been a chimney fire in their street the night the police came to the adjoining apartment and found the body of Joseph Stephano under the floorboards in the unoccupied room. Marianne was in her room, standing at the window watching the firemen and the crowd in the street. Then she saw the police arrive and come into the building. She thought the fire had leapt over the street and would come down into their flat. She began to cry.

Otto came and comforted her. He said a fire couldn't leap that far, it wasn't a kangaroo. He put her back into bed and told her to go to sleep, but she didn't go to sleep. She heard people go into the unoccupied room. They were men, talking in low voices. And then she heard it again, that same creaking noise, like a door that opens onto a ghost story. She went running to Otto and Lucie, drinking coffee in the kitchen that always smelled of baking, and refused to leave them.

She sat on Lucie's knee, with her face buried in Lucie's thick hair. Otto went to listen to the 'noise' in her room and when he returned he looked all around the kitchen, as though searching for something. Marianne believes now that he was searching for words.

Then they heard Joanna Stephano screaming.

'*Otto,*' says Lucie, holding Marianne tightly to her, '*shouldn't we do something?*'

'*No,*' says Otto. The screaming goes on and on.

'*We must do something!*' says Lucie. '*Go, Otto!*'

Otto opened the apartment door, which gave directly into the big kitchen where they sat. Marianne turned round and looked.

She doesn't know now – has never known – whether she saw it, or only imagined it afterwards and then kept on seeing it in her mind: the body of Joseph Stephano being carried down the stairs. She knows only that when she understood what had happened she felt the horror of it every night for years. She'd lie in the dark, biting her nails, imagining it. It had happened just a few feet from her bed. The body of Joseph Stephano had lain right there, squashed into the space between the joists, the boards nailed over him like the lid of a coffin.

Later, when Marianne was grown up and working in her profession, the three of them used to talk about it together. By then, the fear was gone.

'*He used to kick and beat her, Otto,*' says Lucie.

'*I know,*' says Otto, '*but why is the revenge of women always so final?*'

'It has to be,' says Lucie.

'I'm sometimes asked to kill,' says Marianne. *'As an act of mercy. But I tell my patients, I heard the aftermath of a murder once. I'm not the person to ask.'*

Marianne is half asleep. Her hair is washed and dry. She hears a plane go over and imagines the American far above her, flying away from what he did to her and from what he believed Europe was doing to him. Confused Europe. Confused America. She lets him go. She doesn't want revenge. All she longs for is to return to her independent life.

Her telephone is ringing.

At first, she thinks, it's not for me, someone has got the wrong room. Then, because it goes on and on ringing, she picks it up.

'Hey!' says a familiar voice. 'Got you at last. Just got back from the States this morning and I've been calling your hotel all day.'

'Who is it?' says Marianne.

'Who is it? Who *is* it? Are you serious? It's Nico. What's the matter with you, Mother? Have you forgotten you're in the old city?'

'No,' says Marianne. 'Of course not. How could I forget a thing like that?'

Ice Dancing

Ice Dancing

Let me tell you about our house first. Then I'll talk about us and the kind of people we are.

Our house is in Maryland, USA. Our local town is called Cedar, but we're nine miles from there, out on our own, facing a creek. We call the creek Our Creek and I built our house at the edge of it, with every window looking towards the water.

I'm an architect. Retired now. This was my last big challenge, to arrange this house so that wherever you are in it you get a glimmer of Our Creek. Janet, my wife, didn't believe I could do this. She said: 'Don, what about the rooms at the back?' I explained to her that there wouldn't *be* any rooms at the back. 'Sweetheart,' I said, 'think of the house as half a necklace and the water as a neck.' The only thing that's at the back of the house is the front door.

Our Creek flows towards the mighty Chesapeake Bay. On summer evenings, Janet and I stand on our jetty, hand in hand, sipping a cocktail and watching the water slide by. Sometimes, we don't talk. We just stand there watching and sipping and not talking. We've been married for thirty-seven years and now here we are in the place of our dreams. I began life as a clerk. Janet began life behind a Revlon counter.

And we've travelled the world. We started life as dumb Americans, but we didn't stay that way. We've been to England and France and Sweden. And Russia. We've got a whole heap of memories of Stockholm and Moscow. In Stockholm, we visited Strindberg's apartment. We saw his bed and his inkstand and his hairbrushes. He used these brushes to fluff out his hair because he was embarrassed about his head. Not many Americans know this, that the great playwright Strindberg had a tiny little pinhead he was ashamed of.

In Moscow, we witnessed a multiple wedding. We were standing in the snow. The doors of a gray building opened and out of them came a stream of brides, arm in arm with their bridegrooms. It was February. Ten degrees below. And the brides were wearing thin dresses of white net and carrying blood-red bouquets. Janet never got over this sight. Years later, we'd be lying in bed and she'd say: 'Remember those Soviet brides, Don? Out in the cold like that.' It upset her somehow.

And yet winter is her favourite season. The year we moved into this house Our Creek froze. We woke up one morning and there it was: all the water normally headed for the Bay was frozen stock-still. We stood together at our bedroom window, gaping. We were snug in there, on account of the triple glazing I'd had fitted. I put my arm around Janet and held her to me and her body was warm as pie. 'Don,' she whispered, 'let's go out there. Let's go out and dance on the ice.'

I said: 'What d'you mean, dance? We don't have any skates.'

'I don't mean skate,' she said. 'I mean *dance*.'

So that's what we did. We went straight out there before breakfast. We got dressed up in Russian hats and our winter coats and our snow boots. We were sixty years old and we started singing and waltzing on the ice! We sang any old tune that came into our heads, but neither of us has got a voice and we'd forgotten most of the words, so the whole darn thing was crazy. And then, in the middle of it all, as we kept slipping and tripping and laughing, I had this vision of Strindberg. He was standing in the sky, staring down at us. And he wasn't smiling. So I quit laughing and I said to Janet: 'That's enough. Time for breakfast.'

'Oh why, Don?' she said. 'This is *fun.*'

'It's also suicidal,' I said. 'We never thought about that.'

The thing I'll tell you about next happened in Cedar.

Cedar is a smart little Maryland town with three banks and two churches and an avenue of limes along Main Street. There isn't one single cedar tree in it.

We were on Main Street when this thing happened. I'd been to my bank and Janet had been in the hardware store, buying a hoze nozzle. It was a spring morning. The limes were coming into leaf and I stood on the sidewalk looking at Janet about to cross over to me and thinking, here she comes, my Revlon girl.

She walked to the middle of the road and stopped. Then she fell down. She lay in the road. She didn't try to get up.

I ran to her. I could see a truck coming towards us. I put my arms out, waving it down. Other people came running. I knelt down and held onto Janet. Her eyes were open and her face was yellow-white.

'Honey,' I said, 'what happened?'

She held onto me. Her mouth opened and closed, opened and closed, trying to make words, but no words came out.

'OK,' I said, 'it's OK, it's OK . . .'

I sent a boy on a skateboard to call for an ambulance. There was a whole cluster of people round us now. I had to ask them politely to step back, to give Janet some air, to give me room to lift up her head.

We got her to the hospital. The doctors were confused. They said: 'It may have been a mild epileptic seizure. We're not sure. We'll do some tests. Meanwhile, she's fine. You can go see her.'

She was pink again and sitting up in bed. She was wearing a hospital gown, tied at the back. She took my hands in hers. She said: 'I'm sorry, honey. I thought I was back in Danesville, that's all.'

Danesville, West Virginia, was Janet's old home town. Her Dad worked in a glass foundry there. Her mother had raised four children on a foundryman's wage and sent the only girl, Janet, to Beauty School.

After two days at the hospital, they sent Janet home. They told me: 'We can't pinpoint anything at the present time. It isn't epilepsy. Let us know if she has more falls.'

We went home. We had to drive through Cedar, past the exact spot where Janet had fallen down, and I knew I would never go by this place without remembering Janet lying in the road. I thought this would be the thing that would trouble me most in the weeks to come.

But the weeks to come were like no other weeks in my whole life. Boy-o-boy.

The Janet I took home from the hospital was the Janet I knew, but right from this day the Janet I knew started to slip away from me.

She went back into her past. Not all the time. Sometimes, she was right there with me and we'd play a sensible game of rummy or do the crossword or go down to the jetty together and listen and watch for signs of spring. And then, without any warning, bang, her mind got up and walked away someplace else. Mainly, it walked to Danesville. She'd say: 'Don, the temperature on the foundry floor is one hundred thirty degrees fahrenheit. Daily temperatures of this kind burn up a person's life.' Or she'd think our kitchen, with all its built-in appliances, was her mother's old kitchen and she'd complain about soot. She'd say to me, in a simpering voice like her mother's: 'Modern detergents are not designed to cope with old-fashioned problems.'

Sometimes, talking to her would help and sometimes it wouldn't.

Sometimes, if I sat her down and stroked her head and said: 'Janet, you are *not* in Danesville, sweetheart. You are here in the home I built for you, all safe and sound,' she would come out of her trance and say: 'Sure, Don, I know that. You don't need to tell me.'

Then it could happen, too, that she mistook me for one of her brothers. I'd say: 'I am not Charlie, Janet. Charlie was bald, remember? I've got hair like old Strindberg, wild and fluffy.' But she'd refuse to believe me. She'd say: 'You're Charlie. You always were a prankster. And who's Strindberg?'

She got clumsy. She'd always been a meticulous woman. Now, she dropped things and spilled her food and burned her hands on the stove. I said to her one day: 'Janet, I can't stand this any more.' I left the house and went down to the jetty and got into the little canoe we keep tied up there and paddled off down the creek in the rain. I started crying like a baby. I hadn't cried since I was an office clerk.

They operated on Janet on June 30th. It was a hot morning.

Her condition is called hydrocephalus. Water builds up inside the skull and presses on the brain. If the water can't be drained off, parts of the brain atrophy. Then the person slips away – back into the past or to any place where she can't be reached. The success rate of the operation to drain off the water is variable according to age. About thirty per cent of those operated on die.

Death, to me, has always been synonymous with falling. This is how my mind sees it; a long, black, sickening fall. And Janet saw it the same. I once asked her.

Before Janet's operation, the surgeon came to see me. He said: 'Go home. Dig the yard. Mend a fence. This is a long operation. She's in our hands now. There's nothing you can do.'

I said: 'Sure. I understand.'

But I didn't leave. I sat on a chair in a Waiting Area and concentrated my mind on holding Janet up.

I held her in different ways. I carried her above my head, holding her waist and her thigh. When this got tiring, I put her on my back – her back to my back – and her legs made an arc around mine. Then I flew her above me, my hands on her tummy. I stood her on my shoulders and hung onto her feet …

People came into the Waiting Area. They looked at magazines. They read the words 'Ford' or 'Toyota' on their car key tags. They didn't bother me. They recognised that I was busy.

To help me, I sang songs in my mind and I whirled Janet around in time to these. I dressed her in a floaty kind of dress to make her lighter in my imaginary arms. As the hours passed, she got younger. Her hair hung down like it used to when she was a Revlon girl . . .

Then someone spoke to me. It was the surgeon. He seemed to have learned my first name. 'Donald,' he said, 'I'm pretty sure your wife's going to make it.'

They kept her in hospital quite a long while. Then I took her home and the summer passed and then the fall and now here we are again in the winter and this morning we woke up to find Our Creek covered with ice.

Every day, I watch Janet. I watch and wait, for the least sign that she's slipping back to Danesville, but none comes.

She's in fine spirits, too, keen to do things. She says we should travel again, see more of the world before we leave it.

Today, we dress up warm and go down to the creek and Janet says: 'Come on, Don, look at this great ice! Let's dance and fool around on it like we did before.'

She's at the end of the jetty. She's all ready to climb down onto the frozen water.

But I can see that this ice is pretty thin. It's not like it was in that other winter, two foot thick; it's a different kind of ice.

So I call Janet back. I say: 'Honey, don't go down there. It's too dangerous. Enough dancing already. Right? Just stay up here with me.'

Negative Equity

On the night of his fortieth birthday, Tom Harris dreams about a flotilla of white ships.

For a while, he enjoys this dream and feels safe in it. He's admiring the ships from a distance, from a dry cliff. He's wondering, lazily, if they're taking part in a race and looks past them for a fluorescent marker buoy.

The next moment, he realises he's no longer safe. He's in the water, in among the flotilla. He's trying to swim and call out at the same time, but he knows that his head's too small to be seen in the rough water and that his voice is too feeble to be heard. He dreams that he's about to die and so he wakes himself up and still feels frightened and says to his wife Karen: 'Actually, they weren't ships. They were dishwashers and ovens. They were kitchen appliances.'

Karen is Danish. She is forty-three. Her voice is as gentle as a nocturne. She says to Tom in this soft voice of hers: 'I think it's rather peculiar that they should be floating like ships. Would they do that? Is it their hollowness?'

'I don't know,' says Tom, holding onto Karen's hand. 'Perhaps they would float for a while, like empty oil drums, if their doors were shut.'

'But I can't imagine it,' says Karen. 'Ovens bobbing around on the waves. In my mind, they would certainly go down to the bottom.'

Tom and Karen lie silent for a while, just touching. It's a May morning, but their bedroom window is small and doesn't let in much sunshine. The house where they live has always been dark. Tom's mind has now let go of the dream and is concentrated on the realisation of being forty. But he notices that the figure 4 is ship-shaped, and he wonders whether somehow, at forty, a man loses ground and has to set sail for a new place. Karen listens to the noisy summer birds and says after a while: 'I dreamed about the new house.'

'Did you?' says Tom. This house is their future. They refer to it as the Scanda-house because they're building it to a Danish design, with warm pine floors and solar heating.

Karen gets up and puts on her white dressing gown. 'I think I'm going to go and see how the builders are getting on today. Shall I?'

'Yes,' says Tom. 'Why not?'

Then they hear Rachel get up and start talking to her cat. Rachel is twelve and their only child. She has long, smooth limbs and long, smooth, bright hair, like Karen's. Tom, who is dark and small, often finds it strange that he lives his life in the company of these two tall women who are so beautiful and so fair. It's both wonderful and difficult. It's like living with two all-knowing angels.

Tom Harris is a diver. His official title is Coastwatcher. His territory is a ribbon of sea bed ten miles long and a mile wide and his task is to examine this area for signs of life and death. He knows his job is an important one. The periphery of every living thing can yield information about the health of the whole. He was told this at his interview. 'Consider the tail of the bison, Mr Harris,' they said, 'the fin of a whale and the extreme outer branches of a fir.' And Tom is happier in this job than in any he's had. His tools are those of the archae-ologist – the trowel, the knife, the brush, the memory, the eye – but his site is infinitely more vast and changeful than any ruin or barrow. Anything on earth can be returned to the sea and found there.

He wonders what he will find today, the first day of his

forty-first year. In Denmark, as a child, staying near Elsinore for the summer, Karen found a lapis lazuli brooch in a rock pool. She has been proud of this find, always. And in his nine years as a coastal diver Tom has found nothing as beautiful or as valuable as this. But his discoveries have a private value. Sometimes they're so odd that his mind starts work on a story to explain how they got to be there and this gives him a nervous kind of satisfaction. He used to tell the stories to Rachel, but now, for reasons he's unclear about, they have a harsher edge. And he no longer talks to Rachel at bedtime. She prefers talking to her blue-eyed cat. The cat's name is Viola. 'Viola,' says Rachel, 'quite soon we're going to live in a much more brilliant house.'

Tom drives an old Land Rover to the sea. He leaves early, while Rachel and Karen eat their muesli and talk softly together. This morning, as he drives away from the house, he thinks, suppose I never saw them again? Suppose I could never again wake up with Karen? Suppose Rachel's life were to be lived without me? He's never had any tragedy in his life. He can't imagine how certain kinds of tragedy can be borne.

He follows a similar routine each day. He meets his co-diver, Jason, and they put on their wet suits. They comb the beach for lumps of oil and plastic waste and dead things. Jason is a neat man with a lively smile and an old passion for Jane Fonda. In summer, they occasionally find the drowned body of a dune-nesting lark. Cod come into the shallow water and are stranded by the fierce ebb tide and bloat in death. Tom and Jason note the quantity of bladderwrack, the precise colour of the spume on the breakers and the presence or absence of sea birds. They breathe in the wind. Through binoculars, they examine the sea for trawlers and tugs. Sometimes, vast sections of an oil rig are pulled across the horizon, like a piece of scenery across a film location.

They return to Tom's Land Rover and make notes on their beach observation. Jason always brings a Thermos of coffee 'to keep up the body temperature'. (His idol, Jane, has taught him everything he wants to know about the body). Then, they put on their masks and their lamps and their compressed air cylinders, strap on their instruments and walk to the water, carrying their flippers.

Crashing through the waves always troubles Tom – the bulkiness of them, their roar. They're a barrier to where he wants to be. He's not happy until he starts to dive and then he begins to feel it: the thrill of the sudden silence, of the long, beautiful downward flight into darkness. The light closes above his feet and the world is filleted away. He feels ardent, single-minded, like a man travelling to a longed-for rendezvous. He describes this feeling to Karen as happiness and instead of being offended she's amused. 'It's so *Nordic*, Tom!' she says. 'Really and truly.'

He moves slowly across the sea bed, his meanderings guided by the compass attached to his wrist. Steer north-east and the continental shelf will eventually drop away and leave him poised above the real depths he's never entered. So he goes in a westerly way, remembering to stay quite close to Jason, the sea grass just brushing his body, his lamp like a cartoon wand creating a pathway of colour in front of him. Clusters of tiny brownfish explode into sudden stillness, like spilt wild rice, petrified by its light.

He's hoping for some discovery today, for something man-made, trailing a thread of story. He remembers the megaphone and the thurible. The stories he made up around these have taken on substance in his mind, as if they were events and not inventions.

He keeps swimming west, then, signalling to Jason, north a little, out towards the deep. He finds a rusty camera and a bicycle wheel – nothing of interest. He and Jason measure the areas where the sea grass has died.

And so the day passes. He spends quite a lot of it thinking about his two demanding angels and the Scanda-house he's building for them, so that more light can fall on their hair and on their breakfast spoons.

* * * *

When Rachel has done her homework and taken Viola upstairs ('I don't want her going out at night. She chases birds'), Karen makes strawberry tea and sits at the kitchen table opposite Tom. She warms and warms her hands on the tea mug. 'Tom,' she says, 'you know I went to the mortgage people today?'

'Did you? I thought you were going to see the builders.'

'First the builders. Then the mortgage people about the new loan.'

'And?'

'The Scanda-house can't be finished unless we take out another loan, can it?'

'No. But there shouldn't be a problem. This house is worth far more than we've borrowed, so when we sell it—'

'It isn't, Tom. Not any more.'

'What are you talking about, Karen?'

'They sent a young man back here with me. He looked at this house. Just *looked* at it. Barely came inside. Didn't even go upstairs. He said, "Mrs Harris, there's no question of any further loan. You already have negative equity on this property."'

'Negative equity?'

'It's a term. Nowadays, there's a term for everything you can't quite believe could ever happen. I suppose the term is meant to make it real to you.'

'It's not "real" to me. What does it mean?'

'You haven't heard it? I'd heard it somewhere. Out in the air somewhere. It means the house is worth less than the sum we've borrowed on it.'

'It's not, Karen. We had three valuations.'

'But they were a while ago and now all its value is gone. I mean, like water or something. Or into the same air where all these new terms come from. It has just gone heaven knows where. And so I don't see how the Scanda-house is ever going to be completed now.'

Tears start to fall into Karen's tea. Tom feels a hollow place open inside him and bloat with misery. He reaches out and takes Karen's hand and says weakly: 'You may have been misinformed. They may be quite wrong.' He wishes this moment were a story or a dream. 'I'll look into it, Karen,' he says. 'I'll go into it, love.'

He takes a day off. He talks to the builders, to the mortgage company, to the bank loans department. He is told that the gap between what his present house is worth and what he has borrowed to pay for the new one is now approximately £40,000. The only way the Scanda-house can be finished is by borrowing yet more. But nobody will lend him any more because he can't, now, repay the existing loan. His collateral is used up, suddenly, without any warning, like the compressed air in a cylinder that has no reserve valve. He can't move.

He tells Karen he will find a way. 'What way?' she says. 'Tell me what way.'

'I don't know,' he says, 'but I will.'

They say nothing to Rachel. One evening, she informs the cat: 'Our room in the Scanda-house is going to be right up in the roof, Viola, and we're going to be able to see the sea.'

Tom considers asking Karen to go back to work. She used to be an art teacher. One day, she said: 'I can't do this any more, Tom. These children are too savage for me. In Denmark, pupils are not like this.'

She got Tom's agreement. He could see that the children had no interest in the kind of knowledge that Karen could give. So Karen left the school and stayed at home and painted and now and then made a little money from drawings and watercolours. One of the things promised to her in the new house is a studio of her own. It would have a big, sliding window and a balcony made of steel. And Tom longs to see her in there, working quietly, in her own space at last. He can't ask her to return to teaching. He *can't*. She's forty-three. She wants a sunny house with a studio and her days alone with her painting. It's not unreasonable.

Back he goes, down into the deep, to think, to try to work it out. He moves more slowly than usual over the sea bed, barely noticing what appears in the beam of his lamp. He feels like the victims of his stories about the megaphone and the thurible, caught up in something they never intended, that no one intended, but which happened nevertheless. He retells the stories to himself, to see if they shed light on his predicament:

– *One day, a Scouts decathlon is taking place on the beach. There are scarlet markers out at sea for the thousand metres freestyle. The Scoutmaster's name is Dawlish . . .*

– *One winter's day, a Mass is said out at sea on a trawler for a drowned fisherman. The thurifer is a boy named Marcus Grice who is prone to sea-sickness . . .*

Tom stops and thinks, so much of our life is invention, so much the way we *choose* to see it. I see Karen and Rachel as my bossy angels. Karen sees the lost land of her childhood coming back to her in the guise of a house. The men I work for see this ribbon of water as the conscience of England. In both cases, I have inherited so much responsibility.

– *And so. A boy named Pip (the fair-haired boy Dawlish loves single-handedly in his single bed night after night) is coming last in the thousand metres freestyle. Out at the scarlet marker, Pip starts to panic, to wave his arms, to signal that he's in trouble. Dawlish, wearing his Scoutmaster's heavy shoes, wades into the sea and calls to Pip through the megaphone . . .*

– *And so. At a certain moment in the Mass for the dead fisherman, with twenty-foot waves hurling the trawler about, Marcus Grice realises he is about to vomit. Forgetting everything but his own nausea, he drops the thurible and staggers to the ship's rail. Burning incense falls onto the trawler's wooden deck . . .*

'Oh no,' said Karen, when Tom told her these stories, 'I see the endings. I see tragedy coming. Don't tell me. I hate tragedy, when it's so senseless.'

As Tom swims on, he realises a truth that he's never understood before: he wants, through the design of the new house, to remind Karen that England is only partly a dark place, that it can be calm, not savage, that beautiful light often falls on it. This, in his imagination, is why it matters so much.

His worst fear is that Karen will leave, one day, and go back to a place where she once found lapis lazuli in the water.

Sailing yachts and kitchen appliances: he dreams of them often now. The thing which is nimble and defies the water; the thing which, superseded, might float for a while and then sinks.

Karen gets used to this dream of his. When he wakes and reaches for her hand, she just strokes it gently and says: 'That old dream, Tom. It's so rotten to you. I wish it would go.'

One morning, she says: 'I told Rachel about the Scandahouse. I explained there is nothing we can do. Just make it watertight and wait. She understands.'

And they're being so good about it now, his fair women. Hardly any tears from Karen after that first time; no sulking from Rachel. They've understood what's happened and that's that. In the mornings, when he leaves, there they are, chatting softly together, as if the future were going to arrive today. They eat their muesli. They raise their faces to his for a goodbye kiss, exactly as they always and always did.

He's the one who cries. Nobody sees him do it, not even Jason. He tries not to see himself do it. He dives down to the sea floor and switches off his lamp, so that darkness round him is as absolute as the darkness of the grave, and lets his tears fall. His sobs, through his breathing apparatus, sound unearthly.

He does little searching for human objects any more. He prefers lying in the dark. He's tired of the stories men tell. The only thing he's started to long for is to go beyond the coastal shelf, to go to the true deep, where all the variety of the ocean lives. He's begun to believe – at least with half his mind – that only if he is brave enough, insane enough, to go down into this vast darkness will he find the solution to the problem of the house.

One evening, Tom comes home and hears Karen talking on the telephone to her mother, Eva. He can understand quite a bit of Danish. Karen is telling Eva that she's waiting for her life to change. She says: 'I'm not *living* my life any more, Mama. I'm waiting to start it again, when I've got my studio.'

He sits down dumbly and listens to this conversation. He knows that Eva has offered to lend them money, but that the money offered is nowhere near enough and, even if it were, it couldn't be accepted because it couldn't be repaid. Eva is a kind woman and she has passed this quality of kindness onto Karen.

At supper, addressing both Karen and Rachel, Tom says: 'I want to talk about our situation. I promised you I'd find a way out of it. And I still mean to. I don't want you to think I've just given up.'

'No, Tom,' says Karen, 'you're not a person who gives up.'

'It's not your fault anyway,' says Rachel.

Tom pushes away his half-finished meal and lights a cigarette. He doesn't often smoke and the cigarette tastes old. 'I thought,' he says, 'I would have a word with the insurance company.'

Karen says: 'I don't think the insurers can do anything, Tom.'

'Well,' says Tom, 'they will have some idea about the future – about when the value gap might start to close.'

Rachel is looking at Tom's face intently, as though it were a map of the world. 'Do you think it will ever?' she asks.

'Yes,' says Tom. 'Yes.'

He sees the summer pass. The insurers say that they really do not know when the value gap may start to close and they dare not guess. The temperature of the sea rises and then starts to fall again. Tom promises himself that, before the winter comes, he will do the thing he has planned.

It requires the hiring of a boat. He chooses a Saturday morning in September when the air is bright. As he manoeuvres the boat out of the harbour, he looks back and sees, half hidden by trees, his new house, waiting.

He is four or five miles out when he throws the anchor. He

can see the grey smudge of a ferry going towards Harwich and wonders whether, for some of the Dutch passengers coming over from the Hook of Holland, this may be their first sighting of England. When Karen first saw England, she and her friend Else said together: 'It looks a bit like home.'

He checks his equipment carefully. He knows certain important things are being done incorrectly: he should have a reserve valve on his cylinder; he should not be diving alone.

He lets himself tip backwards into the water and goes down slowly, barely moving his flippers, his lamp directed onto the depth gauge at his wrist. He has no idea how far he has to dive before he starts to see it, the life of the true deep. For the first hundred feet of his fall, there seems to be nothing but himself and the drifting bladderwrack and the bubbling of his own breathing.

But then they start to swim into his light: shoals of silver herring; the brown swirl of an eel; a kite-shaped ray with its dancing tail; the blue bodybags of squid; the fingers of cuttlefish; the first red fronds of deepwater seaweed.

For a while, he hangs still, poised where he is, turning and turning his head so that his lamp beam makes an arc and every arc reveals a new picture. He opens his arms to everything he sees, like he used to open his arms to Rachel when she was a small child. With every suck of compressed air that he takes, his feeling of elation increases.

He goes lower, lower. He's no longer looking at his depth gauge. And then, just ahead of him, he sees a dark mass and feels his body pressed by an underwater current. The mass moves by him and on, and thousands of brownfish rush from its path and Tom knows that something vast is down there with him and he chooses to believe that he's found a whale.

He turns and starts to follow it. He scans it with his lamp, but he can see nothing, only the small fish darting from its path. He wants to touch it, to hold onto it, to become its passenger. He wants it to lead him down. *Only by going deeper and further can anything be solved.*

Tom doesn't know whether he can keep pace. He has to

swim as fast as he can, taking in a lot of air, but he does keep pace until he feels the mass suddenly drop away beneath him. It drops and he's stranded there alone, at some mid-point, foolishly kicking his flippered feet. Then he makes the steepest dive he's ever made in his life. Briefly, he thinks of Jason's face wearing a look of terror, then of Jane Fonda wearing a striped leotard and hanging from a wallbar by her feet, and then of nothing, nothing but the beauty of the dive. It doesn't matter whether the thing that leads him down is a whale or not. It's a whale in his mind, just as the Scoutmaster and the thurifer were real people in his mind. It is something alive which, in its every moment of existence, can express its own individual purpose. He has only to follow it and he will attain perfect clarity of thought. The deeper he goes, the more euphoric he feels.

And then, without warning, he's in darkness. He remembers it from his sea-bed crying, this darkness-of-the-grave, and with a heavy arm reaches up to switch on his lamp. But no light appears. The battery of his lamp is used up.

In a mere few seconds he feels a drunken sickness come on and now he can't say if this darkness is the real, external darkness of the deep sea or only a darkness of his mind. Far, far away, weak and soft, he hears Karen's voice say: 'Oh! This darkness of us northerners, this blackness of ours . . .'

Sick as he feels, he knows that he must take control. Karen must be his light now, Karen and Rachel, there on the dry cliff, in a dry wind, with the sun on their hair.

He starts to swim up. But he's lost all sense of time. For how long has he been following the imaginary whale? And how deep is he? Without a light to shine on his depth gauge, he has no means of knowing.

So one question only remains, the question of equity: is the sum of water above him greater than the corresponding sum of compressed air left in his cylinder, or is the sum of the air greater than the sum of the water? He says it like a mantra, over and over, to calm him, to keep his sickness in check: *Which is greater? Which is greater?*

Somewhere far above him his bossy angels wait in the bright September sun and all he can keep trying to do is swim upwards to meet them.

Bubble and Star

Leota Packard had been born and raised in Georgia, not far from Jimmy Carter's home town of Plains. But when she was twenty, she left the South and never returned.

Once in her subsequent life – during the Carter presidency – she found her mind wandering like a lost child back to her mother's porch swing; and there it sat for a few minutes, rocking to and fro, watching the fields. Above the fields, it saw creatures dancing in the air – gnats and fireflies. But this wasn't its usual habit. If Carter hadn't become President, it might never have gone back. Because normally it stayed in Canada, where Leota lived after her marriage to Eugene Packard, a Canadian plastics manufacturer. It stayed in the bright and tidy house Packard built for them two miles from Niagara Falls. It was perfectly happy there and seemed to have no need or inclination to remember the past.

But then, when Leota and Packard were old, when the plastics company had made them rich, when they had lived together for fifty years, the subject of Georgia came back suddenly into Packard's head. Not into Leota's head, but into Packard's. He began saying to strangers at parties: 'Leota is old enough to remember slavery.' The mouths of the strangers would gape and their eyes turn towards Leota, but she would ignore them and look at Packard through the purple sun visor she wore in all weathers and say: 'Those people were not *slaves*, Pack.' And he would reply: 'They were not free, neither, Leota. And that's the truth.'

He was getting angry with the world.

Leota watched him through her visor and wondered when this anger had started.

She decided it had begun the day they went to the unveiling of a painting.

He said to her as they set out: 'Take off that frigging visor, Leota! You see the world through cough linctus.'

She replied: 'I like it that way, Pack.'

'OK,' he said, 'but it's not the way it *is*!'

'How can you say what way it *is*? Everyone sees it differently.'

'Not me,' he said, 'not any more. I see it as IT IS!'

The painting was black. They sat with friends and neighbours in two rows in the town gallery and looked at it and there it was, a black square on a beige background with nothing in it but black, black. The gallery had raised $100,000 to acquire it and yet it looked completely and utterly worthless. Leota had taken off her visor, but as they all sat there in silence she put it on again so that there would be a new kind of magenta colour to the border of the black square.

The artist was introduced to the audience. His name was Pethcot and he wore round black glasses, like pebbles. He smiled and preened and was about to begin to talk about his marvellous square when Packard stood up and said: 'I guess I always knew your world was hollow. Now I get it; it isn't only hollow, it's filled with crap.'

He walked out of the gallery and Leota followed him. For all that day and most of the night, he sat on a chair with a board over his knee, playing Solitaire and mumbling: 'Cheats and liars! Don't *speak* to me . . .'

There was a side of him which had always been down on things, hard on things, including himself and the factory. Asked what the factory made, he had often replied: 'We make trash and the cans to put it in.' He knew 'plastic' wasn't a popular word; it was a word Canadians worried about. Leota reminded him: 'If you manufactured from wood, Pack, they would worry about the trees, but everything has to be made of something.' He answered that anxiety wasn't always rational, any more than despair was rational. 'Who's talking about despair?' asked Leota. 'Everyone,' said Packard. 'Every soul alive.'

This didn't seem rational to Leota. She reminded Packard that one of the products made by the factory was an incubator housing. She said: 'The parents of those babies in your incubators may have been in despair for a while, but when they see their babies aren't going to die they're happy as birds.'

'Nah,' said Packard. 'Wrong. You don't see to the heart of things, Leota. They're happy as birds *for a while*, only until they remember how easily it was going to come.'

'How easily what was going to come?'

'Death. The whole vanishing thing.'

'Pack,' said Leota, 'stop it. You're a normal man, not a poet. Get your mind on something real. Think of the Blue Jays and the great season they're having!'

'I don't give a fly's arse for the Blue Jays,' said Pack.

'Why not? Baseball used to be your craze.'

'Well, it's not any more. I'm through with baseball.'

Leota thought: it's OK to be through with a craze if you can replace it with something else, preferably another craze, even something as trivial as TV game shows. Crazes kept people alive. If you didn't care one way or another about anything, you died. She reminded Pack that Burt Lancaster had kept birds in Alcatraz and this had helped him to go on living, day after day. But Packard only laughed: 'That dates you, Leota! You saw that film in black and white. It predates your visor.'

She didn't mind being teased. Pack was a large man. Large men were often teases. And she'd lived with him for fifty years, just the two of them, no children, no pets, and survived it all and still loved him. But she decided she did mind him getting angry with the world. She minded it for two reasons: 1. she knew that anger takes all the fun and joy out of everything, and 2. it made her feel guilty. It made her wonder whether she shouldn't start to be angry too – whether anger, when you got old, was the only appropriate emotion left. And she'd always been very accepting of the world, never analysed anything with care. Even in her dreams of Georgia, she saw fireflies, not black workers in the fields with their backs bent. It was shameful when she thought about it. And the people who *were* angry with everything – like Steve Cairns, the seven-teen-year-old son of their neighbours, who fought with his father and stole from local stores and left vomit in the driveway – made her frightened. She couldn't help it. Steve Cairns terrified her, him and everybody like him, all the angry punks and bullies. She wanted them to leave Canada. She wanted to send them to the frozen moon.

She lay beside Packard and looked at his white hair on the pillow. She'd noticed, at the unveiling of the black square, that his hair had started to stick out crazily from his head, stiff and wild, as if electricity were fizzing through it. She supposed that fury could generate an electrical charge. Electricity could be made by unexpected things, like the left front door handle of her car, which gave her a slight shock each time she touched it. If Packard's hair got too straight and startling, it might be time to take him away somewhere, to one of the islands in the Hudson Bay, where there was nothing to feel angry about, no charlatan painters, no trash in the water, no TV news of wars and homelessness. Or, she might advise him, simply, to go to the Falls.

Pack had been raised within sight of them and had said all his life that he was 'proud to know the Niagara'. It was there that he went when something upset him. He frequently reminded Leota, when he returned from these expeditions, that 3,000 tons of water *per second* went over the lip. He said: 'Most people in the world live hundreds of miles from any astonishing thing. They don't feel wonder any more. They don't know *how* to feel wonder. And it is wonder, Leota, and that alone that keeps man in check. I'm telling you.'

He didn't need to tell her, really. She could remember watching the stars over Georgia and everyone on the porch saying they felt small and insignificant. And it wasn't as though the subject of the Falls didn't crop up when people visited them from America or England, because it did. One of Packard's favourite pastimes was to re-tell the stories of the stunters, the people who had tried to defy the Falls in barrels or other contraptions 'of their own pathetic making'. Packard despised the stunters, 'the boobies', as he called them, for trying to make profit from the Falls.

He denied that they were brave. He said: 'What's brave about trying to grab notoriety?'

The visitors always listened attentively. They seemed enthralled by the stunts. Leota assured them: 'You don't have to take Pack's view of the matter. He knows it's not the only view.'

'Nah,' he said, 'but it's the only sane view. Take that guy, Stephens, from England. You know what that booby did ? To try to keep his barrel the right way up, he stuck a hundred-pound anvil in the base of it and tied his feet to the anvil and his arms to the lid of the barrel . . .'

Leota always thought, at this point, that she could see the guests trying to remember what an anvil was. She thought an anvil was a hard kind of thing to picture any more. But Pack had pictured it so many times he had no difficulty and he always went straight on. 'You can see what's coming, can't you?' he said. 'That stupid guy! When the barrel went over and hit the water, the anvil dropped out the bottom, wham, in the first second. And Stephens went with it. All except his right arm! And that's the only bit of him they ever found – his damned arm!'

'Oh, no!' the guests would say, 'Oh, God! Oh, my!' And Packard would smile. 'Stephens was the arch booby,' he'd say, 'but there were others. You bet.'

* * * *

Packard always referred to Steve Cairns as 'The Deli'. The nickname amused him. 'You get it, Leota? It refers both to the word "delinquent" and to the quantity of Russian salad he and his friends leave on the neighbourhood walkways.'

He'd always sympathised with Mr and Mrs Cairns, said, heavens, if kids are like that, thank God we don't have any. But now, in his new fury with so many things, he started to invite The Deli into the house for coffee and a smoke. Leota would come into the kitchen and find The Deli sitting with his feet on the table. Occasionally, she made Pack his favourite malted milk and stayed to listen to the conversations. She learned that the Deli's body was slowly being covered with tattoos; he had a woman's breast on each knee, a jewel-handled dagger going from his pubic hair to his navel and a raptor on his back. He offered to show them, but Leota said: 'That's kind of you, Steve, but no thank you, dear.'

Later, she said: 'It's pathetic, Pack. It's so juvenile.'

'Sure,' said Packard, 'but he's looked at the grown-up world and he doesn't like it enough to join it. And who can blame him?'

'That's the way young people always were,' said Leota, 'but they used to want to do something to change it. Now, they just sit around and do things with needles.'

'They see the world's not susceptible to change any more,' said Packard. 'It's too far gone. Even here in Canada. There's no decent people any more. So steal from them. Why not? Governments steal. Big Business steals. Packard Plastics steals . . .'

'Hush,' said Leota. 'Stop thinking that way. I can't endure it. We've only got a few years . . .'

'Exactly. So let's wise up. Get rid of your visor. Let's see things as they are.'

Leota stood up and put her hands on her hips the way her mother used to do when she told off the black maid. 'Packard,' she said, 'I am taking you away.'

The travel agent found her a cabin on an island in the Hudson Bay. It had its own landing stage and a sixteen-foot fibreglass boat. Firs surrounded the cabin and came down to the edge of the water. It was beaver country. The light from the north was fierce.

'OK,' said Packard, when they arrived on a late afternoon, 'this is all right'.

Outside their bedroom, which faced south over the water, was a wooden balcony. Packard found two faded deck chairs and set them out side by side. 'Up here,' he said, 'we will really be able to see the stars. And by the way, dear, stars are silver, sometimes yellowish, sometimes quite white, but they are never purple.'

He got two blankets for them and bought a bag of donuts from the only bakery on the island and there they sat, on their second night, eating donuts and staring at the night sky. It was early spring and cold and silent. Packard tucked the blankets round their knees and Leota took off her visor.

Packard said after a while: 'I read someplace the galaxy's in the shape of two fried eggs, back to back. We're in amongst the white.'

Leota said: 'Astronomers try to simplify everything for us, but the things they ask us to imagine are still pretty darned hard.'

Packard laughed. This was a sound Leota hadn't heard for a while. Then he said: 'I like the way the stars mock us. They're more merciless than the Falls. The Falls are *there* at least, but up there . . . we think we're looking at solid worlds, but we're not, we're looking at travelling light.'

'Why does it stop travelling?' asked Leota.

'What?' said Pack.

'Why does it stop at a fixed point? Why doesn't it come on and on until it gets so close to us it blinds us?'

'It wouldn't blind you, Leota. You'd just be in among a sparkling bilberry soup!'

Pack hadn't noticed that Leota had taken off the visor, but now he did and he held out his hand, sticky with sugar, for her to hold. 'I'm sorry,' he said. 'And for the way I am now. I don't know why light stops travelling. And I don't know why

I'm so darn mad about everything. I guess I'm just a booby, like all the rest.'

'No you're not,' said Leota.

'Anyway,' said Packard, 'I'll be up there in a while. The dead turn into interstellar gas, I bet they do. See that very bright, cold star – that one?'

'Yup. I see it.'

'Look there for me. It's a waterfall star, must be. I think it's called Sirius. My gas particles will be popping somewhere there.'

'Hush up, sweetheart,' said Leota, 'this is a vacation. So why not live for now?'

But he didn't live another day.

He went out in the fibreglass boat at dawn and a west wind blew in from the Northern Territories and the boat over-turned. Packard's body wasn't found for seven days. It had been washed ashore on an island so small it was inhabited only by gannets and geese, who pecked at his nose and at his eyes and at his white hair. The police said to Leota: 'We don't advise you to see the face, ma'am. Identification from the feet and hands will be sufficient.'

Leota had never known loneliness. She never could have imagined how much time it consumed. She'd sit for hours and hours, with her chin on her hands, doing nothing and *being* nothing, except lonely.

It was not only her years with Packard that she sat there remembering – the building of their house, the summer parties they used to give, their mall shopping, their trips to Europe and the States, their love of Cajun food, and all their early years of passion – but her long-ago childhood slowly gathered shape and colour in her mind, like a developing photograph. Her former self felt weightless, or else winged, like the gnats she'd seen at the time of Jimmy Carter. It floated above the landscape, but what it saw were all the ways the people round her were anchored to the earth. She saw all their endeavour. It never ceased. They struggled and laboured and fought until they died. She said to her friend, Jane: 'I may have misunderstood it, but I don't believe these people were angry with the world. I think they loved it to death. But Pack, in his last years, he was so mad at it all. So now I'm confused as well as heartbroken. I don't know which of them was right.'

Sometimes, when the nights got warmer, Leota went out into the yard. She sat on a white tin chair and looked at the sky. She was searching for the bright waterfall star Packard had showed her. She moved her head in an arc, like a searchlight. She took off her visor. She ached for Pack to be alive again and by her side, eating donuts, and to show her the star she couldn't find.

In her solitude, she found it difficult to eat. It was as if there were interstellar gas in her stomach – Lonely Gas, she called it. And so she began to get smaller and narrower and lighter. Even her head. Jane said to her: 'It's not possible that the head of a person can shrink.' But Leota showed her the band of the visor, which she had had to alter by one notch. She said: 'If Pack can die in a boat before breakfast, anything is possible.'

She was now seventy-three years old and had no idea what to look for or how to order the world for the remainder of her life. She knew she couldn't spend it sitting at a table with her chin on her hands or out in the garden in a tin chair. But the fact remained, she was lost without Packard, literally lost. She had difficulty remembering the route to the hairdressers. Driving the car made her anxious, as if it was going to take her some place that she didn't recognise and didn't want to go. She didn't know, at any one moment, what book she was reading or whether she was enjoying it or not. She had to look up the times of the TV game shows she always used to watch. When she stared at the yard, she thought it looked peculiar, as if someone had arrived in the night and moved the shrubs around.

In her kitchen, she listened to the radio. She knew it was important to continue to be told what was going on in the outside world, not least because then she could try to make up her mind about Pack's anger with it. She learned from a radio programme that tigers were disappearing from India, killed by poachers, who sold the bones, ground to bags of dust, to the Chinese. She forgot what the Chinese used the dust for. She was informed that a growth industry in Russia was the sale of human hair. She found these things both disturbing and reassuring; people would do no matter what to stay alive, to buy another week, another day. But then she thought: it's a shame to kill a tiger or sell your hair for another day; and I have days and weeks and years already bought and I don't necessarily want them all. It would be better for those people to be given some of *my* time.

She knew her thinking was confused. In her narrowing head, her brain was probably getting smaller. Grief for a person or a thing could uncouple the logical part of your mind from the rest of it. In Moscow, there could be women who were going insane, grieving for their hair.

She sighed at all this. Her sighs had become insubstantial and sounded like the whispers of a child. She told herself that she had to make a plan, find a goal, or else her future would be completely and utterly blank and dark like the black square painting in the town gallery.

One afternoon, The Deli came round. Leota hadn't seen him since Packard's funeral, where she'd noticed that he had a new tattoo in the shape of a heart on his neck. He brought some limp flowers wrapped in paper and laid them on Leota's kitchen table.

'Thank you, Steve,' she said. 'Sit down, dear, won't you?'

It was summer now and The Deli was wearing a sleeveless T-shirt and torn shorts, exposing the breasts on his knees. Leota could smell sweat on his skinny body. She didn't want him there.

He said: 'I should have come sooner, Mrs Packard. I'm sorry I didn't.'

'Oh, no,' said Leota, 'there was no need . . .'

There was a long silence. Leota thought: Pack used to keep Cokes in the refrigerator for when he called.

'Can I get you a drink of water?' she asked.

'No thanks,' said The Deli. 'My parents told me you didn't get out much any more, so I came to say . . .'

Leota was staring at the heart on his neck. It seemed to be bordered with lace, like the paper heart of a valentine card.

'I can drive now,' he went on. 'I passed my test. So I thought, if there was any place you wanted to go . . .'

Leota looked up. She felt more surprised by what The Deli had just said than by anything she'd seen or heard since the radio programme about tiger bones.

'Why . . .' she said, falling as she sometimes did into her Georgia drawl, 'that is most kind of you dear, but—'

'I mean it. I'd like to drive you somewhere.'

'Well . . .' she said. 'Well. You know the place I haven't been in a long time is the Falls . . .'

'OK,' said The Deli. 'Sure. The Falls. Why not?'

Later, lying in bed, Leota thought: why did I say the Falls? That was Pack's place. What will I do there except get spray on my visor and fill up with Lonely Gas? The truth was, she didn't want to go any place with Steve Cairns. He might throw up out of the car window. He might kill her with reckless driving. But she knew she'd had to accept his offer. After so long of wanting to ship him off to the moon, this was the least she could do.

So they went on a bright August day in Mrs Cairns' Toyota. The Deli drove very fast with one elbow leaning out the window, as if he'd practised driving for fifteen years. Leota examined the lacy heart on his neck and eventually said: 'Your little heart, dear; it looks very near the jugular vein to me.'

'Yup,' said The Deli, 'it is. It's called a 3.'

'A 3?'

'There are three levels of risk with a tattoo. Most of the body carries level 1 – low risk of any side effect, infection or damage to essential tissue. Level 2 would be, say, medium risk: soles of the feet, which could cause problems through inadvertent reflexology. Then there's level 3: inside of wrist, genitals and neck, just here.'

'Do you like danger?' asked Leota.

The Deli scratched his cropped head. 'I guess,' he said. 'I guess.'

When they got to the Falls, The Deli parked neatly and said: 'Shall I wait in the car, Mrs Packard? Do you want to be alone?'

'No,' said Leota, 'I certainly do not want to be alone. I never would go to the Falls alone.'

They got out of the car and Leota, who felt as frail as a bird, took The Deli's arm. The day was windy, but the roar of the cataract was still huge above the wind. Walking towards it, Leota told The Deli that Packard used to stand on the far right, where the grassy bank of the Niagara River tapers towards the precipice. She remembered that he used to lean far out over the rail and gaze at the translucent jade of the lip where, for an instant, the water still reflects the light before it foams white and is gone. She led The Deli to this exact spot and the two of them looked down. Leota let go of the boy's arm and held tightly to the rail. She thought the wind might easily snatch at her and hold her on an eddy above the spray, before letting her fall.

After only a few moments, The Deli said: 'When you get here, when you see it again, you have to admire those stunters, don't you, Mrs Packard? Imagine going over the edge in a barrel? Holy shit!'

Leota said: 'The first person to try it was a woman. Did you know that, Steve? She was called Annie Taylor and she'd been a schoolteacher.'

'Did she make it? Did she survive?'

'Yes, she did. I think it was in about 1901. She was a heroine for a while, till people just forgot about her. And that's the trouble with stunts. People's memory for them is short.'

'Well, I admire those stunters. I couldn't do it. Could you, Mrs Packard?'

Leota stared for a long time at the great spectacle that

Packard had been so proud to know and which had comforted him with its grandeur. Eventually, she said: 'I don't
know, but if I did I wouldn't want to be locked in a barrel in
darkness. I'd want to go over in something transparent – like
a giant bubble – so that I could see everything and know what
was happening to me every second of the trip.'

That evening when the stars came out, Leota made herself a
Martini and took it out into the yard, where she sat down on
the tin chair. She'd given up looking for the waterfall star,
but she chose a black space in the sky and imagined Packard
as a cloud of Lonely Gas within it. The Martini tasted fine.
'Pack,' said Leota, 'you were wrong about Steve Cairns. I do
believe you were – and so was I. Steve was just going through
a *craze* for hating the world, as anyone could, but it's lessen-
ing.'

Leota finished the Martini. She didn't know why Martini
glasses had to be so small.

She took off her visor and looked at Packard's invisible gas
cloud with an unprotected eye. 'He's learned to drive,' she
continued. 'That takes application and you wouldn't bother
with driving lessons – that's what I think, anyway – unless you
planned to go someplace and see some sights. And then,
Pack, he told me he admired the stunters. He doesn't see
them as boobies. Not at all. He sees them as brave people. So
there you are. You thought you had an ally in Steve and I
thought I had an enemy and both of us were wrong.'

As she went back into the house and made herself a second
Martini, she felt defiant, as if something had at last been
resolved. But when she woke up the next morning, she didn't
know why she'd felt this. Nothing was resolved. She'd seen
another side to The Deli's character, that was all. She was
relieved of the burden of referring to him as The Deli and of
wanting to send him off to the moon. But the fact of Packard's
anger still remained. And now she saw, for the first time, that
it may have had a dimension to it that she'd never acknowledged: in coming to despise so much in human endeavour,

he must also have come to despise her. He'd seen how inadequate and false was her vision of her Southern childhood, how unenquiring her Georgia mind. He'd nagged and nagged at her to take off her visor. He'd told her a hundred times that she failed to see things *as they are, Leota*.

She felt bleak. She wanted to say to Pack: I disapprove of killing something as beautiful as a tiger, to grind its bones to some dust or other, of course I do. And a world where women have to sell their blood or their hair or their bodies to buy bread can't be a just place. Even I can see this. And I've always seen it.

No, says Pack's voice. Don't lie. Even now, when you should see the past as it was, you see gnats and fireflies and golden light. You've insulated yourself, with the money I made from trash, with your house in a good clean neighbourhood, with the sweet shade of purple you've coloured all the seasons …

The word 'trash', among all the vexing words of Packard's, was the one that started to haunt Leota most. She looked round her house. It was orderly and warm and comfortable, with quite a few objects of beauty in it. And it was built on a plastics fortune. It was built on products Packard had found worthless.

Leota went into the kitchen. She stared at all the plastic appliances, each with its one and only function of saving her labour and time. And she thought: if I could just see what all the time had been saved *for*, then I would know what to do with the rest of my life.

She couldn't see. She sighed her child-like sigh and began putting her dirty washing into the machine. These mundane things had to be done, even though a person felt bewildered and lost. In a Moscow kitchen, a young woman ties a scarf round her head and puts bones into water for a soup. She does it because she has to go on.

But why go on? Why?

Leota didn't hear Steve knocking at her back door. Or perhaps she heard? Perhaps she said 'Come in, Steve'? She didn't remember. All she knew was that Steve was suddenly there in her kitchen. He was leaning against the washing machine, talking about Japanese cars. Then Leota said: 'Steve, fill the powder dispenser for me, will you, dear?'

'Sure,' he said. But he didn't fill it. He held the round plastic powder dispenser in his hand and showed it to her.

'Look,' he said.

'At what?' said Leota.

'At this,' said Steve. 'You've got the perfect blueprint here – for your Niagara bubble.'

She hardly wanted to let Steve out of her sight after that. She said: 'I know you have to attend school, dear, and smoke and play music and so forth, but you've masterminded the rest of my life and I want you to supervise the plan every step of the way.'

He said: 'You're not serious, are you, Mrs Packard?'

'Call me Leota,' she said, 'from now on. And, yes, of course I'm serious.'

They sat at her kitchen table, drinking Martinis and making drawings. She said: 'We have to remember, Steve, the priority is visibility.'

'And strength,' he said.

Leota said nothing.

He was good at calculations. He said the only thing he could do at school was Math.

'What about History?' asked Leota.

'Trash,' he said. 'Isn't it?'

They measured Leota and weighed her. Her head had shrunk another notch on her visor and her weight was down to 101 pounds. She was the size, Steve said, of a twelve-year-old person.

It was autumn already – six months since Packard's death – when Leota and Steve drove in Mrs Cairns' Toyota to the plastics factory and Leota asked to see the manager, Ron Blatch.

'Ron comes on breezy,' said Leota to Steve, while they

waited on imitation-leather chairs for Ron to appear, 'but his home life's a mess.'

He came in smiling and shook Leota's hand and said it was always a pleasure to see her. She introduced him to Steve and he was, as she knew he would be, courteous to him. She was glad, nevertheless, that Steve was wearing a polo neck that day and that Ron couldn't see his tattooed heart so close to the jugular.

She told Ron Blatch that she was funding a stunt, an attempt to shoot the Falls in a plastic bubble, and that she wanted the factory to make the bubble according to a preliminary design.

Steve produced the drawings that now showed a contraption five feet in diameter and built of transparent air-filled tubing, laid in a circular coil and encased in a clear plastic ball. At its top was a watertight escape hatch that could be opened from both inside and out. Bolted to the ball was a harness made of plastic fibre.

Ron Blatch took out his glasses and put them on. He stared at the drawings. Then he smiled and took his glasses off again and shook his head.

'Stunting's illegal now, the whole length of the Niagara,' he said. 'It's banned absolutely.'

'We know that, Ron,' said Leota. 'We know that . . .'

Ron looked at Steve. 'So who's planning on breaking the law?'

'Well . . .' said Leota.

'No one,' said Steve. 'This is not for personal gain or glory. It's gonna be for charity and charity stunts can be allowed.'

'Ah-huh?' said Ron. 'Like which charity?'

'The aim,' said Leota firmly, 'is to do something in memory of Packard. He was a good man. He minded about the world and Packard Plastics have made life better for thousands of people.'

'Sure,' said Ron.

'But he was unquiet,' continued Leota. 'He was afraid that Canadians had lost their reverence for the natural world, for the things they can't contain and control . . .'

'The Falls are contained OK,' said Ron, smiling. 'Seventy-five per cent of their power is taken by the hydro-electric companies.'

'I know that,' said Leota, 'but still they're not quite tamed, are they? And, to Pack, they came to symbolise all the things he was afraid we'd lost.'

'I know he loved the Falls,' said Ron, 'but I can't break the law for him and you haven't mentioned which charity you're doing this for.'

Leota looked at Steve. She hoped his mathematical mind was working on a formula. After a moment's silence, he said: 'It's to help the old, Mr Blatch. The old are a despised group these days. It's to benefit them.'

Ron rubbed his eyes. He said nothing, but put his glasses on again and stared at the drawings in his hands. Leota thought that he wasn't really looking at them, but only pretending to look at them while he decided what to say and do.

'Ron,' she said, 'Pack was good to you, wasn't he? Fair to you all, wasn't he?'

'Yes.'

'So build this for him. Will you? And don't ask any more questions?'

Ron Blatch looked up. His expression was blank and dumb and Leota felt suddenly sorry for him. He might have liked to go home and talk this over with his wife and get her opinion on whether or not he was about to break the law, but his wife had run off with her fencing teacher and that was that.

'OK,' said Ron.

Leota knew that it would take the company some time to manufacture the bubble. Special moulds would have to be made; Steve's calculations would have to be fed into the firm's computers. So she also knew that she had time to think carefully about what she was planning.

The nights were getting cold. She laid her light-boned body on the couch and listened to a little light Schubert and tried to weigh her own death against the sweetness and beauty of the music.

She decided there must be some sort of balance between wanting to live on and wanting to leave the world in a bubble. Yet what I *see* is the bubble. Only that. I don't see any future at all. The future of Leota Packard is as empty of everything as a Pethcot square. The future is a chair and me on it and my head on my hands.

She dozed and dreamed. The lighter her frame was becoming, the more she floated on sudden little currents of sleep.

One evening, she woke to find Steve in her living room. He was sitting on her Persian rug, rolling a cigarette. When she focused on him, she saw that he looked pale and anxious.

'Leota,' he said. 'Something terrible's happened.'

'All right, dear,' she said. 'Wait here.'

She went to the kitchen and made two Martinis. She came back into the room and gave one of them to Steve. She sat down opposite him and the two of them sipped the drinks in silence for a moment.

Then Steve said: 'They're sending me away.'

'Away?' said Leota. 'Who is and where?'

'My parents. To some frozen school up near Alaska. My dad says he can't stand the sight of me another day. I think it's my knees that freak him out. The tits expand when I sit down. I guess you noticed?'

'Yes, I did, dear. And your mother?'

'She doesn't say anything. She clings on to Dad's arm. He says every line that's on her face I've put there.'

'I haven't noticed many lines. She's a good-looking woman.'

'I know. But that's what Dad says.'

'When are you leaving, Steve?'

'Next week.'

'Well, I'm very, very sorry. A frozen school near Alaska sounds like an awful place. And you're very thin. I'd better give you some of Pack's old woollen sweaters to take with you.'

'Thanks,' said Steve, 'but what about the bubble?'

Leota sat very still and looked around her room and then out of the window, where a November rain was falling.

'I don't know, dear,' she said. 'I don't know. But you're the one we must worry about.'

That night, Leota couldn't sleep. She blamed herself for what was happening. For so long, she'd wanted to send Steve to an icy place outside her world and now he was going there. She'd willed it, out of fear and loathing, and now that all her fear and loathing had gone her will had started to prevail. 'Leota,' she whispered aloud, 'you see everything too late.'

Pointless to cry, she thought. Crying's for the boobies. So she decided to get up. It was two in the morning and cold in the house. She put on her peignoir and her satin slippers frayed at the heels and went out into the yard. She looked up at the sky and there, in the south, was the waterfall star. She remembered its name: Sirius.

It seemed almost blue, the coldest, bluest star in the galaxy. And it was large, as if it were nearer by hundreds of years than all the stars that surrounded it. Leota felt amazed that she could have searched for it for so long and not found it. It blinked at her – light refracted through time and the thousand imaginary cataracts of Packard's mind. And then she heard Packard's laugh exploding up there in its swirl of gas. 'Stars *move*,' he said, 'and the world moves. You've never understood how each and every damn thing in the universe is changing every second of time. So from where you stand, Leota, this is a winter star.'

'OK, Pack,' she heard herself say, 'I see it now.'

She'd always been an impatient person. As a child, when she woke before dawn, she used to yell at the sun to come up. And once she'd decided on a thing, she wanted to make it happen straightaway.

At eight, she called Steve and asked him to come by. He arrived at nine with his roller skates round his neck. Leota made coffee.

'Steve,' she said, 'I've seen everything all wrong.'

'What do you mean, Leota?'

'Well. I don't need the bubble after all. You see? It was typical of me to think about a bubble, to think about plastic protection, just like my old visor, but I don't need it.'

'What are you going to use, then? A barrel?'

'No. I'm going to use nothing.'

'Come on . . .'

'It's what I want to do. You won't be able to put me off, so don't try. I'm a Georgia girl and stubborn. But I need one last favour from you, dear.'

'Leota . . .'

'I want you to drive me there. If I went alone, I could lose my nerve. And I want to do it tonight. It has to be night, because I don't want to petrify any Japanese or French tourist. And tonight feels good to me. So if your mother would very kindly lend you the Toyota . . .'

Steve got up. He put his roller skates on the floor and lit a cigarette. He walked to the window and smoked silently for a moment, then he turned and said: 'I want to be absolutely clear what you're telling me.'

'I'm telling you that I'm sorry,' said Leota. 'Sorry for everything. Sorry for all the things I didn't properly understand and sorry, in particular, that you're being sent away to the moon.'

'It's not the moon,' said Steve.

'Near,' said Leota.

'It's not enough,' said Steve. 'It doesn't explain it.'

'Well, it's too bad,' said Leota. 'That's all I can say. That's it.'

He arrived in a pick-up truck. He said: 'The days when I can borrow the Toyota are gone.' He told Leota that the pick-up belonged to the father of a bass guitarist.

Leota had chosen her outfit carefully: clean white underwear and white socks; blue-pants, bought at Queens Quay, Toronto; a white silk blouse and a pale-blue wool jacket with a little silver monogram on the pocket; white shoes she normally only wore in summer. She'd washed and combed her short white hair and fixed two jade earrings to her still soft ear lobes.

'You look nice,' said Steve.

'Thank you, dear,' said Leota.

When they left, towards midnight Leota didn't look back at the house that Packard had built for her and where, she had to admit, she'd been foolishly happy. She kept her eyes straight ahead on the moonlit road and all her mind was on the tiny particle of the future that remained. She and Steve didn't speak until they turned off the main highway leading to the Falls and started down an old track that led nowhere but in amongst some trees and stopped at a barbed-wire fence. A hundred yards beyond the fence was the Niagara River. 'I know this,' said Steve, out of the darkness, 'it's a place where I've been.'

Leota didn't ask what he'd been here for. Instead, she said: 'It's so very kind of you, dear, to help me in this way. I hope you won't get into any kind of trouble on my account.'

'Don't think about that,' said Steve.

He stopped the car and they both got out. They were some way upstream from the Falls, but they could hear them, even *feel* their nearness in the ground underneath them. They stood very still, holding onto the truck. It was a cold, cloudy night with no stars.

Leota had been precise about the arrangements she wanted. She would walk on her own through the trees to the water's edge. She would wait there a few minutes. Meanwhile, Steve would drive back onto the highway and park up in the Falls parking lot. Then he would go and stand at the rail – exactly where they had stood on their visit – a few feet from the lip of the waterfall. He was to carry a strong flashlight. With the flashlight, he was to scan the water, looking for Leota's bobbing head, and, when he found it, he was to fix the light on her. 'Your light,' she'd said, 'will be the last thing I see and it will be like a star. You must be certain to follow me all the way, till I'm over and gone.'

They hung back by the truck, getting cold, because neither of them knew how to say goodbye. So then Leota just started to walk forwards, without a word. She was at the fence and climbing through when Steve called out: 'Wait! Leota, wait a minute!'

She was on the other side of the fence now. Steve ran towards her and, with the barbed wire between them, put his arms round her. She was much smaller than him. She reached up and put a kiss on his tattooed heart.

At the water's edge, she took off her shoes. She felt no fear at all. 'None, Pack,' she said. 'So there you are.'

She was impatient, in fact, to get into the surging green river. Her only worry was that her body was too light to fall straight down under the guillotine of water. She thought it might reach the lip and go flying outwards – as once had happened to a young boy – and arrive in the pool below still alive. But this was a small risk. No one else had survived the Falls without the protection of a barrel.

She let time pass, but then she didn't know how much of it had gone. She'd heard Steve drive away in the truck, but she couldn't tell whether he would have taken up his position at the lip yet and switched on the flashlight.

She waited five more minutes, gauging the time by counting. Then, she put her white shoes side by side and got into the water.

It was so cold, it took her thoughts away. And the current was far stronger and wilder than she'd imagined. She was like flotsam in it, being whirled round like a fairground car. Waves broke over her and her mouth filled with water. She choked and spat. She tried to hold her head high, to swim properly, to grab her thoughts back. She'd believed that the green river would be easy and lead her gently to the edge, but it fought her, as if jealous of her destination, as if it wanted to claim her before she reached the fall.

With her bony hands, with her legs in blue pants, with her neck and chin, she fought its intention. Each time she surfaced, she could see, to her delight, the yellow beam of Steve's flashlight directed at her from the bank. As long as that light was there, she believed the river wouldn't take her. And when she knew at last that she was there; when, in the final second, she felt the water become calm before it slid her over and hurled her down, she found a voice to raise against the thunder. 'Hey!' she yelled. And it was to Leota as if all the world could hear her and would remember this moment of hers for years and years to come: 'Watch this! The last booby!'

John-Jin

When I was a child, the pier was a promising place.

You walked along and along and along it, with all its grey sea underneath, and at the end of it was the Pavilion.

'Now,' my father used to say, 'here we are.' He was a person who enjoyed destinations. Inside the Pier Pavilion were far more things going on than you could imagine from the outside; it was like a human mind in this one respect. You could drink tea or rum or 7-Up in there. You could play the fruit machines or buy a doll made of varnished shells. You could shoot at a line of tin hens to win a goldfish. You could talk about your life to a fortune teller or ride a ghost train. There was a section of the great glass roof from which flamenco music came down. And under the music was a Miniature Golf track.

My father and I used to play. Our two miniature golf balls followed each other over bridges and through castle gates and round little slalom arrangements until they reached their destination. This destination was a wishing well and every time we played both of us had to make a wish, no matter who won the game. My wishes changed with time, but I know now that my father's did not. I wished for a pair of wings and a trampoline and a pet reptile and flamenco dancing lessons. My father wished for John-Jin.

Then, when I was ten, the Pavilion detached itself from the pier in a storm and moved five inches out to sea.

I remember saying: 'Five inches isn't much.' My father replied: 'Don't be silly, Susan.' My mother took my hand and said: 'It's a building, pet. Imagine if this house were to move.'

They closed the whole pier. Things separated from their destinations can become unsafe. When we went down to the beach, I used to walk to the locked pier gates, on which the word 'Danger' hung like an advertisement for an old red car, and watch the tugs and cranes dismantling the Pavilion bit by bit. They towed it all away and stacked it on a car park. Their idea was to raise all the money it would cost to bring it back and rebuild it and join it onto the pier again, but no one said when this would be.

It was the year 1971. It was the year I got my flamenco shoes and began my Spanish dancing lessons. It was the year that John-Jin arrived.

He was Chinese.

He'd been left wrapped in a football scarf in a woman's toilet in Wetherby. He'd been found and taken to a hospital and christened John-Jin by the nurses there. How he came to be ours was a story nobody told me then. No one seemed to remember, either, what colour the football scarf was or if it had a team name on it. 'The details don't matter, love,' said my mother, changing John-Jin's nappy on her lap; 'what matters is that he's with us now. We've waited for him for ten years and here he is.'

'Do you mean,' I said, 'that you *knew* he was going to come?'

'Oh, yes.'

'So you had someone waiting in that toilet all that time?'

'No, no, pet! We didn't know *where* he was going to come from. We never thought of him being Chinese necessarily. We were just certain that he'd arrive one day.'

He was as beautiful as a flower. His eyes were like two little fluttering creatures that had landed on the flower. If I'd been an ogress in a story, I would have eaten John-Jin. I used to put his flat face against mine and kiss it. And I entertained him when my parents were busy. They'd put him in a baby-bouncer that hung from a door lintel and I'd get out my castanets and put on my flamenco shoes and dance for him. The first word he ever said was *olé*. When he learned to stand up, he went stamp, stamp, stamp in his red bootees.

'Don't wear him out, Susan,' said my mother. 'He's only one.'

'I'm not,' I said. 'I'm helping him get strong.'

When he was in bed sometimes, with his gnome night-light on, I'd creep into his room and tell him about the world. I told him about the building of a gigantic wall in China and about the strike of the school dinner ladies. I told him about the Miniature Golf and the wishing well. I said: 'The Pier Pavilion was there and then not. There and then not. And that happens to certain things and I don't know why.'

Making the pier safe took two years. People in our town were asked to 'sponsor a girder'. You could have your name cast in the girder and then you would be able to imagine the waves breaking against it. I liked the idea of the sea breaking against my name, but my parents decided that it was John-Jin who needed his own girder more. They said: 'You never know, Susan. Doing this might help in some way.'

We needed help now for John-Jin. Something was going wrong. He could do everything he was meant to do – talk, bounce, walk, laugh, eat and sing – except grow. He just did not grow. Nobody explained why. Our doctor said: 'Remember his origins. He's going to be a very small person, that's all.' But we thought that was a poor answer.

We kept on and on measuring him. He grew in minute little bursts and stopped again. When he was three, he could still fit into the baby-bouncer. I wanted to buy him his first pair of flamenco shoes, but his feet were too small. At his nursery school, he was seven inches shorter than the shortest girl. The little tables and chair were too high for him and the steps going up to the slide too far apart. The nursery teacher said to my mother: 'Are you seeking advice from the right quarters?' And that night, my parents sat up talking until it got light and I went down and found them both asleep in their armchairs, like old people.

The next day, we all went out in an eel boat to see John-Jin's girder bolted onto the pier. John-Jin kept trying to reach down into the eel tank to stroke the eels; he wasn't very interested in his girder. My mother and father looked exhausted. It was a bright day and they kept trying to shade their eyes with their fingers. I thought the girder was beautiful – as if it had been made in Spain. It was curved and black and John-Jin's name stood out in the sunlight. This was one of the last girders to be put in place. Our eel boat was anchored right where the pavilion used to be. And so I said to John-Jin: 'Pay attention. Look. Without your girder, they couldn't have finished mending the pier.' He blinked up at it, his straight, thick eyelashes fluttering in the bright light. Then he turned back to the eels.

'Where are they going?' he asked.

My parents took John-Jin to a specialist doctor in Manchester. Every part of his body was measured, including his penis and his ears. My mother said: 'Don't worry, Susan, he's far too young to feel embarrassed.'

A course of injections was prescribed for him. He had to go to the surgery every week to get one. I said: 'What are they injecting you *with*, John-Jin?'

'Something,' he said.

'Just a growth hormone, dear,' said my mother.

I was going to ask, what is a 'growth hormone'? Where does it come from? But a time in my life had come when I couldn't carry on a conversation of any length without my thoughts being interrupted. The person who interrupted them was my flamenco dancing partner, Barry. He was fifteen. He wore an earring and a spangled matador jacket. When I danced with Barry, I wore a scarlet flamenco skirt with black frills and a flower from Woolworths in my hair. And so, instead of asking more about John-Jin's growth hormones, I went dancing with Barry in my mind. I replaced the subject of growth hormones with the smell of Barry's underarm deodorant and the sight of his shining teeth. I knew my mind was a vast pavilion, capable of storing an unimaginable quantity of knowledge, but all that was in it – at this moment in my life – was a single item.

And then, John-Jin began growing.

We measured him against the kitchen door. When he got to three feet, we gave a party, to which Barry came minus his earring and danced with John-Jin on his shoulders. John-Jin had a laugh like a wind chime. Barry said when he left: 'That kid. He's so sweet. In't he?'

'Now we can stop worrying,' said my mother. 'Everything's going to be OK. He'll never be tall because his real parents almost certainly weren't tall, but he'll be much nearer a normal size. And that's all we were asking for.'

I know something important now. Don't ask for a thing unless you know precisely and absolutely what it is you're going to get and how you're going to get it. Don't ask for the old Pier Pavilion back. There's no such thing as the old Pier Pavilion. There will only be the *new* Pier Pavilion and it will be different. It will not be what you wanted in your imagination. My parents asked for something to make John-Jin grow. They didn't ask what that 'something' was and nor did I. And together we allowed in the unknown.

It took some time to show itself. It took ten years exactly.

I had become a dance student in London when I first learned about it. In a cold phone box, I heard my father say: 'We waited so long for another child. I used to wish for John-Jin at the end of every game of Miniature Golf. Remember that?'

I said: 'Yes, Dad. Except you never told me what it was you were wishing for.'

'Didn't I? Well, never mind. But . . . after all that . . . I never, Susan . . . I mean I never thought about the possibility of losing him.'

'Shall I come home?' I said.

It was near to Christmas. John-Jin was twelve years old. He lay in bed without moving. His curtains were drawn, to rest his eyes, and he had his old gnome night-light on. He said it reminded him of being happy. His speech was beginning to go, but he wanted to talk and talk, while he could still remember enough words. He said: 'Suze, I can't hardly move a toe, but I can still chat, *olé!* Tell me about the world.'

I said: 'Here's some news, then. Remember Barry?'

'Yes.'

'Well, he's in prison. I went to visit him. He stole a van. He remembers you. He sent—'

'If you don't love him any more, it doesn't matter,' said John-Jin.

'No, it doesn't,' I said, 'but he was a good dancer.'

I sat in a chair by John-Jin's bed and he stared up at me. His face-like-a-flower was smooth and creamy and undamaged. After a while, he said: 'I've had it, Suze. Did they tell you?'

I took his hand, which felt cold and heavy in mine. 'Not necessarily,' I said, but he ignored this. He knew every detail about his disease, which had been named after two German scientists called Creutzfeldt and Jacob. It was called CJD for short. It had been there in the growth hormones and had lain dormant in John-Jin for ten years.

He explained: 'The hormones come from human glands. The chief source of pituitaries used to be the mental hospitals – the cadavers no one minded about – and some of these died of CJD. Mum and Dad are going to sue, but it's much too late. Someone should have known, shouldn't they?'

'Why didn't they?'

John-Jin shook his head. He said: 'I can still move my neck, see? I can turn it and look at the room. So why don't you get a flamenco tape and dance while I can still see you. You could become a star, and I would have missed it all.'

I found the music and an old pair of castanets. I put on a black skirt and fixed a bit of tinsel to my hair. I was ready to begin when I looked down and saw that John-Jin was crying. 'Sorry, Suze,' he said. 'Get Mum to come and clean me first. I've no control over anything now. I live in a fucking toilet.'

In the dark December afternoon, I walked out along the pier on my own, along and along it to where it ended at the deep water.

I imagined John-Jin's girder underneath me. I wondered, in my rage, if you took that one piece away, would everything fall?

Trade Wind
Over Nashville

It was July and hot. At six in the morning, vapour rose from the tarmac parking lots.

'Know somethin', Willa?' said an Early Breakfast customer at the counter of *Mr Pie's* restaurant. 'You look so pretty in that waitress cap, it's like yore dyin' a' beauty!'

'I declare!' said Willa. 'I never heard such a thing in the world!'

The waitress cap was lace. Polyester and cotton lace. Then there was the gingham dress that Willa had to wear. With that on, you didn't see the last days of her thirtieth year passing. No, sir. What you saw were her pushed-up tits and the waist she kept trim and the sweet plumpness of her arms. And as she handed the early customer – one of her 6 a.m. regulars – his plate of egg, sausage and biscuit, he took all of her in – into his crazed head and into his belly.

She lived in a trailer in a trailer park off the airport freeway. Her lover, Vee, had painted the trailer bright staring white, to keep out the Tennessee sun. Willa had a Polaroid picture of Vee with his paint roller and bucket, wearing shorts and a singlet and his cowboy boots. She nailed it up over her bunk, just low enough to reach and touch with her stubby hand. Shoot! she sometimes thought, what kills me dead 'bout Vee is his titchy short legs! And she'd lie there smiling to herself and dealing poker hands in her mind so as to stay awake till he came home. And then, when he did, she'd whisper: 'Vee? That you, Vee, wakin' me up in here?'

'Who else?' he'd ask. 'Who else you got arrivin'?'

'Well then?'

'Well what?'

'Why ain't ya doin' it to me?'

So, on the next lot, at two in the morning, frail Mr Zwebner would wake to hear them shouting and pounding the hell out of their white walls. Zwebner had dreams of Viennese chocolate. Patisseries eaten with a little fork. And what he felt when Willa and Vee woke him was an old, unassuagable greed. 'That Willa,' he'd sigh, 'she's got it coming to her. She's got something, one day soon, gonna come along.'

At *Mr Pie's,* she poured coffee, set up a side order of donuts next to the plate of sausage. Seeing her arm reflected in the shiny counter, she said: 'Lord! Ain't that a terrible sight, the elbow of a person. Look at that, will ya?'

The customer looked up. His mouth was full of egg. He stared at Willa's arm.

'If Vee ever did see that, how wizened an' so forth it is, well, I swear he'd leave me right off. He'd jes take his gee-tar and his boots an' all his songs an' fly away.'

The man wiped his jowls with a chequered napkin. 'He sold any a' his songs yet, that Vee?'

'No. Not a one.'

'Then he ain't gonna leave ya yet.'

'What's that gotta do with him leavin' me or not?'

'Got everythin' to do with it, Willa.'

'I don't see how.'

'Only one thing'll make him quit, honey. And it ain't no piece a' your elbow. It's fame.'

Willa stared at the fat customer with her wide-apart eyes. Trouble with a place like *Mr Pie's,* she said to herself, is everyone stick their noses in your own private thoughts.

Out at Green Hills, in the actual hills that looked away from *Mr Pie's* and all the other roadside diners and all the gas stations and glassed-in malls, lived Lester and Amy Pickering.

Lester was a roofer. He'd started small and poor, working out of a garage in East Nashville. Now, he was halfway to being rich. Halfway exactly was how he thought of it, when he drove down Belle Meade Boulevard and past the Country Club and saw and understood what rich was. And at fifty-two, he'd begun to wonder whether he'd get there, or whether this was how he'd remain – stuck at the halfway point.

'Lester, you know, he's tiring,' said Amy to her friends at the Green Hills Women's Yoga Group. 'I see it plain as death. It's like he's up against a wall and he just don't have the go in him to climb it. It's like gettin' this far took all the vim he had.'

'Well, Amy,' the friends would reply, 'let him tire, honey. You got a good house an' your kids both in college. What more d'you want?'

'Ain't a question of want,' said Amy. 'It's a question of dream. 'Cos one thing you can't stop Lester doing, you can stop him doing 'most anything 'cept having these dreams a' his. He's the type he'll die dreaming. He's descended from a Viking, see? Got this conqueror still goin' round in his veins.'

On that July morning at six, as more of Willa's regular customers stumbled into *Mr Pie's* and she wiped the counter for them, taking care not to look at her elbow's reflection, Lester Pickering climbed into his pick-up and drove south toward Franklin. He'd been asked to tender for a job on a Baptist church, to replace tin with slates. 'Git out here early, Lester,' the Minister had advised, ' 'for the ole tin git too hot to touch.' And now he was doing sixty-five in the pick-up and his light-weight ladders were rattling like a hailstorm above his head. But his mind wasn't on his destination. He was driving fast to drive away the thoughts he was having, to jolt them out of his damn brain before they took hold and he did something stupid. Thoughts about Amy and the fruit seller. Thoughts about this guy who comes from nowhere and calls Amy up, knows her number an' all, and says meet me at such-

and-such parking lot and I'll sell you raspberries from the mountains. And so she goes and she meets him and for two days she's bottling and freezing fruit and making jelly with a smile on her face.

'Who is he?' asks Lester.

'I dunno,' says Amy. 'Name of Tom. That's all I know.'

'An' how's he got all them berries? Where they come from?'

'From the hills.'

'What hills?'

'He said it's a secret where they precisely come from, Lester.'

'Why's it a darn secret?'

'I dunno. That's it about a secret, uhn? You often don't know why it is one.'

Lester was driving so fast, he missed the turn-off to the church. He braked and saw in the rear mirror a livestock truck come hissing up right behind him. Ready to ram me, thought Lester, because the thing of it is, people don't care any more. They don't care what they do.

While Willa worked at *Mr Pie's*, Vee slept on in the trailer. The sun got up high. Sweat ran down Vee's thighs and down his neck. He was on the verge of waking, it was so hot and airless in the trailer, but he kept himself asleep and dreaming. In his dreams, he was no longer Vee Easton, cleaner and dogs-body at Opryland; he was Vee La Rivière (he pronounced it 'Veeler Riveer'), songwriter to the stars of the whole darn world of Country Music. He was certain this future would come. He was so certain about it, he wasn't really dreaming it any more, he was thinking it up.

'What's the diffunce between dreamin' an' thinkin', Vee?' asked Willa.

'I'll tell ya, sweetheart. What the diffunce is, is between fairytales and actuality. What them things are now is actual.'

'You mean "real", doncha? You mean *re*-ality, Vee. That's the word you were meanin'.'

'If I'd've meant real, I'd've said real. What I mean is, things actually happening, or, like they say in the Bible, Coming to Pass. Vee La Rivière is gonna Come to Pass.'

And when Vee woke, around eleven, he remembered what day it was. It was the day of the night of his meeting with Herman Berry. *The* Herman Berry, known nationwide, but with his heart and his house still in Nashville and a set of his fingernail clippings in a glass case in the Country Music Hall of Fame, right slap next to Jim Reeves's shoes.

Vee thumped his leg and sat up. He got out of his bunk and snatched up a towel and dried the sweat on him, then opened wide the four windows of the trailer and the daytime world of the trailer park came in, like homely music. He put on some blue stretch swimming trunks and made coffee. He didn't give one single thought to Willa or to anything in his life except this big meeting with Herman Berry, when he would play him three songs he'd written. 'Keep it to three, boy,' Herman had said. 'Keep it to a trinity and I'll listen good. More 'an that and my mind starts walking away.'

But which three would he offer? Veritably speaking, Vee admitted to himself, as he turned the pages of his music note book, there's only one of Herman's calibre and that's my new one.

He got his guitar and tuned it a bit. He felt suddenly chilly in his torso, so he put one of Willa's thin old counterpanes round his shoulders. Then he flipped the pages to his new song, called *Do Not Disturb*, and played the intro chords. Then he made like he was talking to Herman Berry and explaining the song to him:

'. . . them ther's just the introductory bars, Herman. Key of C minor. Little reprise here before the first verse. A moody reprise, I call it. Let every person know this is a sad song. Tragic song, in all absolute truth. OK? So here we go with the first verse:

> I went up to my hotel room
> And got some whiskey from the mini-bar . . .

'In parenthetics, Herman, I didn't never stay in no hotel room with a mini-bar, but Willa put me straight on that detail. She said, you can't say "got some whiskey from the bar" just, 'cos what hotel rooms have now is mini-bars, OK? Means adding coupla quavers to the line, but then I keep it scanning in the fourth, like this:

> I set my pills out on the table,
> And wondered how it all had got this far.

'You get "it all", Herm? "It all", that's his life and the way it's turning out.

'So now, another reprise of the opening chords. Still quiet-ish. Still keeping the tragic mood. Then we're into the second verse, like this:

> I thought of you in Ole Kentucky,
> And the singing of the sweet blue grass.
> For a year we'd been together,
> Now you told me, Jim, all things must pass.

'We could change Jim, right? It could be Chuck or Bill, right? Or Herm. It all depends on how you want to personalise it an' make it a true Herman Berry number.

'Anyway, it's the chorus now. Modulation. Big, swoopy modulation to C major here. As we go into the big chorus that all America's gonna be singing soon:

> Believe me, girl, my heart was breaking!
> Breaking tho' I couldn't say a word,
> It was my life I was intent on taking,
> So then I hung the sign out,
> The sign that stopped them finding out,
> The little sign that said Do Not Disturb!

'That's the thing I'm pleased with – the chorus. Whatcha say, Herm? You don't think they're gonna be humming that from Louisiana to Ohio? Before I go to the third verse, tell me how you feel about that big, sad chorus. You don't gotta speak. Just stick your thumbs up.'

* * * *

Amy Pickering knelt down on her Yoga mat in her living room and folded her large-boned body into a small, coiled position called the Child Position. She shut her eyes. She tried to have vacant, childlike thoughts, but these didn't seem easy to come by, because what was in her mind was Lester.

Why did you lie to him, Amy Pickering? she asked herself. Why did you make out there was a secret about the raspberries? When all that guy was, was some friend of Betty Bushel's that likes to bypass retail and sell direct to housewives?

She didn't know the answer. All she knew was she had liked to do it. Lying about the raspberries had made her feel beautiful. It had. She had stood in her kitchen, smelling all that scented fruit, and feeling like Greta Garbo.

Amy lifted her head. She stretched her neck and smoothed her graying hair that she wore in a French pleat. Beyond the sunlit sills of her room, she could hear the peaceful neighbourhood sounds – lawn mowers and birds and Betty Bushel's dog yapping at shadows.

Then, in her mind, she saw Lester, years ago, wearing his old hunting jacket, standing in his father's yard with his father's dog, Jackson, sniffing at his boots. He'd built the kennel for that dog. He'd put on a neat little shingled roof and that was what got him started on the idea of roofs. 'It had a twenty-six year life, that kennel,' Amy liked to boast fondly. 'Two dogs, both named Jackson one after another, lived to thirteen in it. That's how good made it was. But then, Lester's dad, he said to me: "Dogs is heartbreak, Amy. I jes' can't stick to have another Jackson leave me for the Lord!" So I dunno what he did with that kennel then. 'Less he kept it somewhere to remind him of his son . . .'

He was still alive, the old man. The idea of him dying seemed to hurt Lester in his chest. When he thought about his father dying, he'd knead the area of his heart. And this is what he'd done when Amy had told him her lie about the raspberry seller: he'd stood looking at her and kneading his heart through his draylon shirt.

'Oh my . . .' sighed Amy. 'Oh my, my . . .'

'Git through m' shift at two, be home at three,' Willa had told Vee in the night. 'Then what I'll do, darlin', I'll press your shirt and tie and steam out the fringes on your coat, so they fall good. And that way, Herman Berry's not solely gonna 'preciate your songs, he's gonna see yore an upright person.'

'Upright?' Vee had burst out. 'What's upright got to have to do with song writing? You could be a mean, wastrelling bum, an' still make it big in this business, honey. You could be an orang-utan. It wouldn't matter. 'Cos no one's looking at ya. They only listening. They only saying to theirselves, Is this gonna catch on? If I record this *Do Not Disturb*, will it make it to number one in Anusville, Milwaukee?'

Now, as Willa took off her lace cap and changed out of her gingham frock, she told her friend, Ileene: 'You could be an orang-utan an' still make it in Nashville, Ileene. 'Cos the point is, all anyone's got is their eyes closed.'

'Oh yeh?' said Ileene. 'What about here, then? I swear some pairs of eyes go up your ass, Willa, when yore wipin' tables.'

'Well, that,' said Willa, 'but then I ain't singin'.'

Ileene shook her head and smiled as she pulled on her lace cap. 'Darn cap!' She grinned. 'Look like a friggin' French maid in that, don' I?'

'I dunno,' said Willa dreamily. 'Bein' as how I never saw no French maid in my whole existence.'

As soon as she got off her bus at the trailer park, Willa knew that Vee wasn't there, because his car was gone.

'Drove off about half an hour ago with his guitar,' Mr Zwebner said. On hot days, Mr Zwebner sat on a plastic chair in the narrow band of shade made by his trailer, reading some old, mutilated book. Willa could not imagine any mortal life so monotonous as his.

'Thank you, Mr Zwebner,' she said. Then she added: 'Got an appointment with Herman Berry tonight. 'Fore the Opry starts.'

'He famous, then? He someone I should know of?'

'Who? Herman Berry?'

'Yeah.'

'You never done heard of Herman Berry, Mr Zwebner?'

'No.'

'You kiddin' me?'

'No.'

'Shoot! I jes' don't believe what yore sayin'! I don't believe my eardrums, Mr Zwebner!'

'OK. You don't believe.'

'Herman Berry? Why, he's so darn famous, he can't go anywhere without people want to touch him and git bits of him.'

'Why they want to do that, Willa?'

'*Why?* Well, 'cos that's what they wanna do. They wanna touch his fame and have it touch them.'

Mr Zwebner smiled and closed his leatherbound book.

'Have it touch them, eh? Like it's catching?'

'It *is* catchin'. Fame is. I swear. Vee had this friend he used to visit with, who somehow stole a dry-cleanin' ticket offa Dolly Parton's manager or secretary or someone. One Pair Ladies' Pants, Silver. Got it framed an' all in a silver frame. And then fame came to him in the form of he began his own dry-cleanin' outlet in Hollywood, an' now he's doin' shirts for Mel Gibson and so forth.'

Mr Zwebner shook his head. Old folks like him, thought Willa, they never believe one word you tell 'em. Like as if reality ended 'fore you was born. So she told him, have a nice afternoon, Mr Zwebner, and went into her trailer and stood in the dark of it, looking at the two bunks, hers and Vee's, and deciding then and there she'd like Vee in her life for ever. She sat down on his bunk that was still damp from his sleep and smoothed his pillow.

Then, in her quiet voice that had this kind of crack in it, ever since she was a kid and sang *Jesus Loves Me, This I Know* with her head lying on her grandma's lap, she began to sing Vee's new song:

I thought of you in Ole Kentucky,
And the singing of the sweet blue grass,
For a year we'd been together,
Now you told me, Jim, all things must pass.

At Lyleswood, Lester was up on his ladders, measuring the tin roof and the tin-capped belfry of the Baptist church. The Minister stood on the ground and stared up.

'Tin warped a bit, Lester?' he called.

'Yeh. It's warped, John.'

'Gonna look a whole lot finer in gray slate!'

'Cost y'all a whole lot more 'an the tin did, too.'

' 'S OK. We been fund raisin', like I tell you. Auctions. That's the way to do it. Hog auctions. Needlework auctions. Jelly auctions, we even had.'

'Little by little you did it, then?'

'You got it, Lester. Little by little.'

'Same way as I built my business up.'

He was about to smile down at the Reverend, but then and there as he said these words, Lester felt himself falter, like old age had climbed up the ladder and put its hands on his shoulders. He held on to the guttering. Little by little, small contract by small contract, he'd made it to halfway. Halfway between East Nashville and Belle Meade. Halfway to the antebellum-style house he dreamed of with white colonnades and a fruit garden in back, where he'd grow raspberries. But how in hell could he find the strength to make it through the second half? I won't, was his thought. Amy knows I won't, which is why, I guess, she keeps going with that Yoga of hers. Believing, if she can stand on her head, her hopes gonna fall out.

'You OK up there, Lester?' called the Minister.

'Yeh. Coming down now, John.'

Slowly, taking care to feel each rung of the ladder under his shoe before putting his weight on it, Lester descended. He could feel the sun burning down on his bald spot, but his belly was cold.

'Don't it scare you never, bein' up on a roof, Les?'

'No.'

'Guess up there yore nearer to God.'

'Day I'm scared, that's the day I'll quit.'

'How much it's gonna be, then, for the slate roof?'

'I ain't worked it out yet.'

' 'Proximately how much?'

'I ain't done the sums, John.'

'We got four thousand raised. Keep it near to that, an' you'll get the tender. We don't want no big firm comin' in and takin' our money. That's the people's roof, Lester. That's a roof built of crochet and jelly and pies.'

Lester nodded. 'Amy makes a lotta jelly,' he said, 'outta all the summer fruit.'

Willa sat on Vee's bunk a long time, singing. Then she lay down and pulled the damp sheet over her head and went right to sleep.

When she woke, she knew something had changed inside the trailer, so she sat up and stared around and then she got what it was: the hot sun had gone and at the open windows the little thin curtains were flapping about like crazy and the whole air was cold, not like the air of a summer storm, but like the air of winter.

Willa got up and put on one of Vee's sweaters, then closed the windows, snatching the curtains in. She took one look at the sky and swore she'd never seen anything made her more afraid, because the sky was cut in half, half hazy and bright and the other half pitch inky black, and the black half was coming nearer and nearer, like the end of the world was just sliding in over Tennessee.

She wanted to call to someone. She would have even called to Mr Zwebner, but he wasn't outside on his chair. He'd taken his chair in and locked his door, and Willa had the feeling that in the whole trailer park no one was moving.

So she turned on the radio, hoping for some bulletin telling her if the end of the world was coming or not, but all she could get clear enough to hear through the static was the Grand Ole Opry, live, and who was up there singing but Herman Berry. Hearing Herman, she thought, now, soon, I'm gonna feel less scared to my teeth, 'cos Vee's gonna drive home an' be with me.

She sat on her hands on Vee's bunk, listening to Herman Berry sing a Johnny Cash number and hoping Vee wasn't there, at the side of the stage where he liked to be, but in the car already, coming towards her. She didn't care one speck whether Herman Berry had liked *Do Not Disturb*; all she minded was whether Vee was going to get to her before the sky fell down on her head.

'Come on!' she called aloud. 'Come on, Vee!'

She turned the radio down and started listening for a car. But all she could hear was the wind. The wind was getting so bad, she felt the trailer move. She felt it rock, or lean or something, like there was an earth tremor under it.

'Willa,' she said to herself, 'yore thirty years old and yore about to die!' And the weirdest thing was, old Herman Berry just went on singing the song and at the end of it the audience clapped and shouted, like the Opry was far away in another state, where the sky was normal and the sun was going down in a normal way.

'Herman,' said Willa, 'the world is endin', honey. Someone go out an' take a look!'

Lester and Amy Pickering were at supper when they first heard the wind. Then the room got dark and Amy said: 'My! Whatever is happening, Lester?'

Lester had a mouthful of corn bread. Chewing, he went to the window and saw what Willa had seen – the slab of darkness moving over the sky.

'Uh-huh,' he said.

'What is it, dear?'

'Boy-o-boy . . .'

'Lester?'

'Take a look, Amy.'

Amy came and stood beside her husband and looked out.
Then she took hold of his hand. 'God Almighty, Lester! What
the heavens is it?'

'Low pressure. Big low front moving in.'

'Jesus Christ! Looks like a building falling down on us!'

'Severe low. Knock out the power, maybe. Better get us
some candles and a flashlight.'

'Shoot! I never seen such a thing!'

'We got any candles?'

'I guess.'

'Get 'em, then, Amy.'

'*God!* I never in my life saw that.'

' 'S only weather.'

'Don't look like weather, do it? Look like *Apocalypse Now.*'

'Get the candles, OK?'

'Come with me, Lester.'

'Why?'

'I'm scared, that's why.'

'Told you, Amy, it's only weather.'

'OK, so it is. That don't mean I don't have to be afraid.'

'... afraid?' said Willa. 'That ain't the word for what I felt that
night. If I live to be sixty – which I won't, now my heart's got
broke – I'll never be that terrorised. Bad enough it was, I
guess, for folk in houses. But for us in the trailer park, well,
you couldn't imagine how it was, because that wind, it came
and lifted up our homes. It lifted them plumb off the earth,
and one of 'em, the trailer of my neighbour, Mr Zwebner, it
lifted so high, it came down on the Interstate and how Mr
Zwebner didn't die was only because he wasn't *in* his trailer;
he was in mine, tryin' to stop me screamin'...'

The worst thing was, Vee didn't come home.

If Vee had come, Willa could have clung to him and maybe
they would have sung songs or something to keep their fear
from getting the better of them. But the hours passed and full
night came on, and there wasn't a sign of him. No car arriving.
No Vee in his cowboy boots, holding his guitar. Nothing. Just

177

darkness and the screaming, tearing wind and the trailer creaking and moving and the sirens going and all the thin poplars that screened the park from the Interstate snapping in half, like matchwood.

What could Willa do but start screaming?

'Vee!' she screamed. 'Help me, Vee! Vee! Come help me! Vee! Where are ya? Vee! VEE! *VEE!*'

And some time after all that hollering for Vee, there'd been a thumping on her door and she thought, Sweet Jesus, he's home, and she undid the latch and the chain and went to pull him in, to take him in her arms and not let go of him till she died or the wind ceased, whichever came soonest. But it wasn't Vee. It was Mr Zwebner in his thick night clothes that smelled of onion or something, and he began hollering back at her not to scream. 'You make yourself sick with this screaming, Willa, I swear!' he shouted. And he put his smelly hand over her mouth and gripped her arm and shook her like you would shake a chicken, to wring its neck.

And after a moment of this shaking, she came out of her screaming and broke down and sobbed with her head on Mr Zwebner's chest, through which she could hear his old heart still just about beating.

'Mr Zwebner,' sobbed Willa, 'where's Vee? Don't tell me he's gone?'

And then the gust came that pitched Mr Zwebner's trailer onto its end and sent it spinning down onto the freeway.

'Woulda killed him dead,' said Willa, ' 'cept he was with me, helpin' me in my hour a' need.'

Though Amy had found some candles, she and Lester didn't need them, because, by some kind of miracle, the power lines in Green Hills stayed standing.

What came flying off were the roofs. On almost every house on every bit of the green hills, the wind tore in under the shingles and sent them hurtling down.

Lester heard this happen and saw it in his mind's eye – all the roofs just being blown away. And he stayed up all night, sitting in a chair, not afraid of the wind, but just thinking about it.

Near two o'clock, Amy said: 'Maybe we should go to bed. Or at least lie down for a while?'

But Lester shook his head. 'Can't lie down, Amy,' he said. 'Too much on my brain.'

So they sat on in the living room. Amy picked up photos of their grown-up children and looked at them and thought back to how, when they were little, and they had their rickety old house in East Nashville, they used to be afraid of it in a high wind, as if it planned to do them harm.

But Lester wasn't thinking about his children, or about the past. He was thinking about Belle Meade and the future. He was thinking about money.

'Amy,' he said, after some hours, 'know what?'

'What, Lester?'

'This storm ain't gonna hurt us none.'

'I sure hope not,' said Amy.

And then they were silent again. But Lester smiled as he sat there, because he saw what was coming. In a few months – if he stayed cool and cunning and didn't let the pressure get to him – he could make more money than he'd seen in years. Enough to get beyond this halfway point. Enough for the house with the fruit garden and the colonnades.

Only thing was, he wouldn't be able to do the Baptist church. There just wouldn't be any time for that. 'I sure am sorry, John,' he'd say to the Minister, 'but that night of the storm, it changed a lotta things.'

It got light.

The wind mellowed down, and the people of the trailer park stood about, looking at the ruin all around them.

Half the roof was gone from Willa's home, but it was still standing, so she said to Mr Zwebner: 'You have a nice rest, till the police an' all come, Mr Zwebner. You lie down right here, on Vee's bunk, OK, and cover yourself with the counterpane.'

'What will you do, Willa?'

'Ain't nothin' for me to do, really, 'cept go to work. Take my mind offa things. Always supposin' *Mr Pie's* ain't blown away to Kansas.'

So Willa washed her face and hands, wiped all the blotched shadow from her eyelids and put on fresh, and went to wait for the 5.30 a.m. bus, which didn't arrive.

She began to walk. The sky was a kind of dead white colour and there were no shadows anywhere on anything.

As she walked, she thought, I dunno, I jes' dunno what coulda happened that Vee never got home. It's like God said: 'I'm gonna take one on them, Willa. Vee, or the trailer. I'm gonna puff one on them away.' 'Cos what life is, it's *never* all the way you want it. More like half. Like you can have Vee, or you can have your home be one of the lucky ones not destroyed by the wind. But you can't have both.

Soon after Willa arrived at *Mr Pie's*, while she and Ileene were still setting up the relishes and sauces, Lester Pickering came in and sat down at the counter and ordered an Early Breakfast.

He knew Willa by name, for it was a thing he loved to do, to get up early, while Amy was still sleeping, and treat himself to sausage, biscuit, grits, hash browns and egg before he went to work.

'How yo're, Willa?' he asked, with a grin. 'Survive the storm, did ya?'

'Just about, Mr Pickering. Trailer next to mine blew down. You want coffee, sir?'

'Sure. Lotsa coffee. Sat in a damn chair all night.'

'Me, my neighbour done come in to quieten me. I was screamin' so hard, I couldn't hear m'self.'

'Where was Vee, then?' asked Ileene. 'He didn't come back after his big success, then?'

'What "big success"?'

'You didn't listen to the Opry, Willa?'

'Sure. Bits of it.'

'You didn't hear Herman Berry?'

'Yeh. I heard him.'

'Singin' Vee's song?'

'He weren't singin' no songa Vee's. He was singin' a Johnny Cash number.'

'Before that, he sang Vee's song.'

'You was hearin' things, Ileene.'

'No, I wasn't. Tell you the title of the song, if you want: *Do Not Disturb*. Told the audience, "I learned this just today, in one afternoon, 'cos I liked it so much I wanted to sing for y'all tonight. An' it's written by a new songwriter, resident here in Nashville, name of Vee La Rivière."'

Willa put the coffee back on its burner. She rested her elbow on the chrome counter and gave Ileene one of the long, hard stares she was famous for in her childhood.

'You lyin' to me, Ileene?'

'No. I ain't lyin'. *Do Not Disturb*. He ain't written a song called that?'

'Yeh. That's his new one.'

'Well then. There y'are. He's famous now. Vee La Rivière.'

Willa said nothing more to Ileene. She went into the kitchen and waited there while Fat Pete cooked Lester Pickering's breakfast. Then she took the plate of sausage and grits and the side order of donuts and set them up on the counter.

'Everything OK for you here, Mr Pickering?'

'Yes, thank you, Willa.'

'You gonna be busy, I guess, with all them roofs flyin' off?'

'Yeh. Busier than I ever been.'

'What happens, then, to folk as lost their roof? Insurance pays, do they?'

'Yeh. Most everyone's got coverage.'

'That's lucky.' Then she smiled at Lester Pickering, whose mouth was stuffed with sausage. 'Shame I couldn't of had somethin' like that on Vee,' she said. 'Some insurance, like. Know what I mean? So that when his good luck blew in, I was covered. Know what I'm sayin', Mr Pickering?'

Over

Over

Waking is the hardest thing they ask of him.

The nurse always wakes him with the word 'morning', and the word 'morning' brings a hurting into his head which he cannot control or ameliorate or do anything about. Very often, the word 'morning' interrupts his dreams. In these dreams there is a stoat somewhere. This is all he can say about them.

The nurse opens his mouth, which tastes of seed, and fills it with teeth. 'These teeth have got too big for me,' he sometimes remarks, but neither the nurse nor his wife replies to this just as neither the nurse nor his wife laughs when from some part of his ancient self he brings out a joke he did not know he could still remember. He isn't even certain they smile at his jokes because he can't see faces any longer unless they are no more and no less than two feet from his eyes. 'Aren't you even smiling?' he sometimes shouts.

'I'm smiling, sir,' says the nurse.

'Naturally, I'm smiling,' says his wife.

He's being nursed at home in his own small room that was once a dressing room. His curtains are drawn back and light floods in. To him, light is time. Until nightfall, it lies on his skin, seeping just a little into the pores yet never penetrating inside him, neither into his brain nor into his heart nor into any crevice or crease of him. Light and time, time and light, lie on him as weightless as the sheet. He is somewhere else. He is in the place where the jokes come from, where the dreams of stoats lie. He refuses ever to leave it except upon one condition.

That condition is seldom satisfied, yet every morning, after his teeth are in, he asks the nurse: 'Is my son coming today?'

'Not that I know of, sir,' she replies.

So then he takes no notice of the things he does. He eats his boiled egg. He pisses into a jar. He puts a kiss as thin as air on his wife's cheek. He tells the nurse the joke about the Talking Dog. He folds his arms across his chest. He dreams of being asleep.

But once in a while – once a fortnight perhaps, or once a month? – the nurse will say as she lifts him up onto his pillows: 'Your son's arrived, sir.'

Then he'll reach up and try to neaten the silk scarf he wears at his throat. He will ask for his window to be opened wider. He will sniff the room and wonder whether it doesn't smell peculiarly of waterweed.

The son is a big man, balding, with kind eyes. Always and without fail he arrives in the room with a bottle of champagne and two glasses held upside down between his first and second fingers.

'How are you?' he asks.

'That's a stupid question,' says the father.

The son sits by the bed and the father looks and looks for him with his faded eyes and they sip the drink. Neither the nurse nor the wife disturbs them.

'Stay a bit,' says the father, 'won't you?'

'I can't stay long,' says the son.

Sometimes the father weeps without knowing it. All he knows is that with his son there, time is no longer a thing that covers him, but an element in which he floats and which fills his head and his heart until he is both brimming with it and buoyant on the current of it.

When the champagne has all been drunk, the son and the nurse carry the father downstairs and put him into the son's

Jaguar and cover his knees with a rug. The father and the son drive off down the Hampshire lanes. Light falls in dapples on the old man's temples and on his folded hands.

There was a period of years that arrived as the father was beginning to get old when the son went to work in the Middle East and came home only once or twice a year, bringing presents made in Japan which the father did not trust.

It was then that the old man began his hatred of time. He couldn't bear to see anything endure. What he longed for was for things to be over. He did the *Times* crossword only to fill up the waiting spaces. He read the newspaper only to finish it and fold it and place it in the wastepaper basket. He snipped off from the rose bushes not only the dead heads but the blooms that were still living. At mealtimes, he cleared the cutlery from the table before the meal was finished. He drove out with his wife to visit friends to find that he longed, upon arrival, for the moment of departure. When he made his bed in the morning, he would put on the bedcover then turn it down again, ready for the night.

His wife watched and suffered. She felt he was robbing her of life. She was his second wife, less beautiful and less loved than the first (the mother of his son) who had been a dancer and who had liked to spring into his arms from a sequence of three cartwheels. He sometimes dismayed the second wife by telling her about the day when the first wife did a cartwheel in the revolving doors of the Ritz. 'I've heard that story, darling,' she'd say politely, ashamed for him that he could tell it so proudly. And to her bridge friends she'd confide: 'It's as if he believes that by rushing through the *now* he'll get back to the *then*.'

He began a practice of adding things up. He would try to put a finite number on the oysters he had eaten since the war. He counted the cigarettes his wife smoked in a day and the number of times she mislaid her lighter. He tried to make a sum of the remembered cartwheels. Then when he had done these additions, he would draw a neat line through them, like the line a captive draws through each recorded clutch of days, and fold the paper in half and then in quarters and so on until it could not be folded any smaller and then place it carefully in the wastepaper basket next to the finished *Times*.

'Now we know,' his wife once heard him mutter. 'Now we know all about it.'

When the war ended he was still married to the dancer. His son was five years old. They lived in a manor house with an ancient tennis court and an east-facing croquet lawn. Though his head was still full of the war, he had a touching faith in the future and he usually knew, as each night descended, that he was looking forward to the day.

Very often, in the summer of 1946, he would wake when the sun came up and, leaving the dancer sleeping, would go out onto the croquet lawn wearing his dressing gown and slippers from Simpson's of Piccadilly and stare at the dew on the grass, at the shine on the croquet hoops and at the sky, turning. He had the feeling that he and the world made a handsome pair.

One morning, he saw a stoat on the lawn. The stoat was running round the croquet hoops and then in and out of them in a strange repeated pattern, as if it were taking part in a stoat gymkhana. The man did not move, but stood and watched. Then he backed off into the house and ran up the stairs to the room where his son was sleeping.

'Wake up!' he said to the little boy. 'I've got something to show you!'

He took his son's hand and led him barefoot down the stairs and out into the garden. The stoat was still running round and through the croquet hoops and now, as the man and the boy stood watching, it decided to leap over the hoops, jumping twice its height into the air and rolling over in a somersault as it landed, then flicking its tail as it turned and ran in for another leap.

The boy, still dizzy with sleep, opened his mouth and opened wide his blue eyes. He knew he must not move so he did not even look round when his father left his side and went back into the house. He shivered a little in the dewy air. He wanted to creep forward so that he could be in the sun. He tiptoed out across the gravel that hurt his feet and onto the soft, wet lawn. The stoat saw him and whipped its body to a halt, head up, tail flat, regarding the boy. The boy could see its eyes. He thought how sleek and slippery it looked and how he would like to stroke its head with his finger.

The father returned. 'Don't move!' he whispered to his son, so the boy did not turn.

The father took aim with his shotgun and fired. He hit the stoat right in the head and its body flew up into the air before it fell without a sound. The man laughed with joy at the cleanness and beauty of the shot. He laughed a loud, happy laugh and then he looked down at his son for approval. But the boy was not there. The boy had walked back inside the house, leaving his father alone in the bright morning.

Also available from Vintage

ROSE TREMAIN

The Way I Found Her

'Quite simply magnificent . . . *The Way I found Her* is a
magical invention of page-turning suspense, of sadness, grief
and passion, whose sure and delicate exposure of a sensibility
flowering one hot Parisian summer teaches
us the price of experience. Do not miss it'
Elizabeth Buchan, *The Times*

'A scary, funny and ultimately very affecting novel . . .
Tremain lets us glimpse the adult-in-waiting; reminds us that
life – tinged with joy, sex, pain – takes its whole shape from
such moments'
Mail on Sunday

'This novel has the sparkle of sunlight on water . . . Such is
Rose Tremain's skill that she simply bewitches you into
believing . . . You too are in Paris, on holiday, caught up in the
heat and the enchantment . . . once more Rose Tremain
beguiles you into suspending disbelief'
Independent on Sunday

'Surely one of the top 10 novels of the year, with Tremain more
original, funny and captivating than ever'
Elle

VINTAGE BOOKS
London

Also available from Vintage

ROSE TREMAIN

The Cupboard

'Deeply evocative . . . a book brimming with life'
The Times

'Strongly constructed . . . highly relevant . . . thoroughly
fascinating'
Sunday Times

When Erica March composes herself to die in a cupboard she
knows that Ralph Pears will find her. For at the age of 87, she
has told the young journalist the richly colourful story of her
life as novelist, political activist and, above all, lover, from
childhood in Suffolk, Paris between the wars, to oblivion in
post-war London. At the end of Ralph's patient probings only
one secret remains: the mystery inside the one constant object
in her life – her cupboard.

'Rose Tremain has managed to get into the skin of her clever
and wilful old heroine'
Daily Telegraph

'Much of the power of the book springs from Erica herself, a
magnificent and greatly sympathetic creation . . . Miss Tremain
has fashioned the totality of one life – and conveyed the
evanescence of all human existence'
Sunday Telegraph

VINTAGE BOOKS
London

Also available from Vintage

ROSE TREMAIN

Sadler's Birthday

'A rather special work . . . A *tour de force*'
New York Times

'*Sadler's Birthday* is as far from the stereotype of a young
woman's first novel as it can be. It is a masterly study of a
lonely but loyal man that is deeply felt, intelligent and often
touchingly funny. I liked it very much'
Angus Wilson

Today is Jack Sadler's birthday. Or is it? He's not sure, doesn't
care. It might be his last day or the beginning of a new chapter
in his life. He must find the key to his old room. He knows
the truth about his past lies there and somehow he must get
in and confront it.

'A first novel of remarkable talent; never a foot set wrong'
Financial Times

'A quintessentially English writer – her work has a charm and
finesse, a civilised irony'
Guardian

VINTAGE BOOKS
London

Also available from Vintage

ROSE TREMAIN

Letter to Sister Benedicta

'Funny, sad and intensely moving, it is a joy to read from beginning to end . . . Miss Tremain does something to restore my confidence in the vitality of the English novel . . . *Letter to Sister Benedicta* should be seen as a triumph of the human spirit over the afflictions which beset us'

Auberon Waugh

Fat and fifty, educated only to be a wife and mother, Ruby Constad has reached a point of crisis. Her husband, Leon, lies in a nursing home after a stroke that has left him paralysed; her grown-up children are gone. In her anguish Ruby appeals for help to a half-remembered figure from her colonial Indian girlhood – Sister Benedicta. Gradually, the events leading up to Leon's stroke are revealed and a woman emerges whose capacity to love, hope and understand are far greater than she realises.

'An original talent clears the hurdle of a second novel with pathos and humour'

Guardian

VINTAGE BOOKS
London